Comedy

ISBN: 978-1-951226-24-4

Cover illustration: detail of *The Cat* (1607) by Edward Topsell

Author photo by Dean Davis

Published by Trident Press
940 Pearl St.
Boulder, CO 80302

tridentcafe.com/trident-press-titles

COMEDY

Stories by Mathias Svalina

Trident Press
Boulder, CO

CONTENTS

If I suffered what else could I do

    —Bernadette Mayer

LAKE

I cut my hand off on the bandsaw. It just sat there on the workbench. I almost fainted, but then I didn't, so I wrapped a rag around my hand, or my wrist, or my stump, & called 911. I picked up my hand & exited the garage. I sat on the curb. I held my severed hand in my unsevered hand. It looked like the set-up for a joke.

A woman walked up to me with a baby in her arms. "I already called 911," I said. Blood had turned my jeans black & heavy.

The woman handed the baby to me. It was so abrupt. I dropped my severed hand to take the baby. She turned & walked to a blue Dodge Comet & got in & drove away. My rag had loosened on my arm, or my stump, & blood was really coming out again. The blood got all over the baby.

Sirens approached through the neighborhood. The baby began crying.

When the ambulance turned the corner I was starting to lose it. The day was coming to me as if through a glass brick. An EMT came up to me. I handed him the baby. The baby was covered in blood. Things looked bad.

"What's wrong with the baby?" he asked.

"I don't know," I said. "It's not my baby."

"Whose baby is it?" the EMT asked.

"Some lady," I said. "She drove away."

The EMT took the baby back to the ambulance. I waited for my turn. It seemed rude to cut in front of a baby.

Then the ambulance engine started. And the ambulance drove down my culdesac to turn around & head back toward the hospital. As it passed me the driver gave me a thumbs up. I held up my bleeding stump in a kind of salute.

I called 911 again, since the baby took my ambulance. My hand was in the dirt on the street. I picked it up & tried to get the dirt off the blood-parts by rubbing it against my jeans.

The blue Dodge Comet drove up & stopped in front of me, idling. The woman leaned over & rolled down the window. It had one of those old window cranks & her body moved rhythmically as she turned it.

"Where's the baby?" the woman asked me through the window.

"The ambulance came & took it," I said.

"I cut my hand off," I added.

"Well," the woman said, "I need that baby back. I never should have given the baby to you." She was smoking a cigarette & she flicked the butt out the window. When it hit the asphalt it rolled to me & I stamped it out with my shoe.

I fainted then. When I came to the woman was sitting next

to me. The car in front of us, idling. She held my hand in one hand & shook me with the other.

"I'm going to take this," the woman said.

"No!" I said. "It's mine. I need that hand."

"I gave you the baby. It's even-steven," she said.

"But the ambulance guys took the baby."

"Well, that's on you."

Then I fainted again & woke up in an ambulance. The EMT guys were different, which was odd to me at the time. One of them was a woman.

"Where's my hand," I asked the woman EMT.

"It got cut off," she said.

"Yes, but the woman took it," I said. "Where is the woman?"

"I don't know what you're talking about," she said. "Now lie back down. You're losing a lot of blood."

I laid back on the gurney. I couldn't feel my hand. But beyond that I couldn't feel anything. Later I would understand that they'd given me some drugs, but right then I assumed I was dying.

"I'm dying," I told the EMT. She had a package of gauze in her mouth & she grunted something that was not a word in response.

SCHOOL

The first time my son came home from school covered in blood I was concerned. It was not his blood.

The second time, I called the principal to register a complaint. The messaging system was voice activated. After repeatedly saying "Principal Butler" & hearing the mechanized female voice reply, "I'm sorry could you repeat that?" I gave up.

The third time my son came home from school covered in blood that was not his blood I found a chunk of meat hidden in his backpack. The meat was wrapped in pages torn from a science textbook. Faint blonde hairs sprouted from the skin-side of the chunk, like the limp baby hairs my husband grew after using that anti-balding cream.

I decided the chunk must have come from the leg of a girl. I decided I must see the principal. I decided to visit her the next day after I dropped my son off at school.

Parents filled the hallway outside the principal's office. Many spoke to one another about the blood lately covering their children. Some looked sad & were silent. I figured their children were the source of the blood. Other parents stood impatiently, texting violently, snapping at unseen people on the other sides of phones.

The principal's office was still dark, though classes had begun. Some minutes later, a woman wearing dark blue jeans & a cardigan came down the hallway carrying a sheet of paper. She pushed through the parents, pulled a roll of blue tape from her cardigan pocket. & taped the paper to the door.

Parents gathered around after she left. The grumbling increased. Some parents walked away & out the double doors with the wire-laced glass. I jostled forward. In large bold Times New Roman, the paper read "The Principal is DEAD."

I turned to the parent next to me, a man in a suit. He looked at my face. I looked at his face. He asked, "Is this some kind of joke?"

I said, "I can't say."

The man turned to another parent. "Is this some kind of joke?"

I walked down the hallway to the front doors. I put my hand to the bar, but paused. I sent positive reinforcement thoughts to my son. "Be strong," I sent-thought with eyes shut tight. Then louder: "BE STRONG!" Then I yelled my thoughts, "DON'T GET KILLED!" And then "DON'T GET EATEN!"

Back home I logged into the company database & checked emails & tasks. There were few tasks, but I could stretch them out to fill the whole day. Intermittently, I stopped & sent thoughts to my son. "BE STRONG." "DON'T GET EATEN." I opened an email from a co-workers. She had figured out a fix for a glitch. I rewrote the email & sent it to my boss as if I had conceived the fix. Then I stopped, squinted my eyes tight again & thought-yelled "IF YOU HAVE TO EAT THEM, THAT'S OK."

By afternoon my head hurt from squinting. I poured a glass

of wine. I laid my face flat against the kitchen countertop. The marble was cold. I was an airplane flying through a frozen fog. I was a fish swimming beneath the frozen surface of a frozen lake.

My son stood in the kitchen. Chunks missing from each leg. Blood dripped to the linoleum, in clean & dripping notes, like single piano keys, like frozen fog, like ice cracking. He stared at me with bready eyes.

The note of his blood was A-sharp. In real life I'm not good at pitch. But in the dream I knew it was an A-sharp. That was important in the dream.

*

Around three, my son came home. His face was clean but muted remains of blood splatter dotted his clothes. Someone had tried to wash it out.

I debated whether the image of him washing blood out of his own clothes at school was more or less disturbing than him standing naked while an adult—I pictured his science teacher—washed the blood out as the two stood beneath fluorescent lights.

We have a nice room in the front of the house that we rarely use. I call it the parlor. My husband never calls it the parlor. In the parlor is a matching sofa & chair set that I bought because I thought they looked classy. I took my son into the parlor & sat him on the sofa. I sat on a chair.

"I've been having some concerns," I began. "I can't help but notice that you've been coming home covered in other people's blood."

I looked at my son. For a moment I imagined him as a parking attendant at a big garage in a big city, the kind who sits in the little booth all day collecting money & sneaking cigarettes. His face looked like that.

"Also," I continued, "I found that chunk of meat that you brought home yesterday." He remained impassive. "Tell me. Is it human meat?"

"Mo-om," he whined, twisting sideways.

"Don't you 'Mom' me," I said.

He unzipped the small pocket of his backpack. Then he zipped it shut. He did it again, the move calculated to convey impatience.

"Come now," I said. "You would not act like this to your father."

"Dad's never here, so it don't matter. And where is dad?"

I did not want to talk about his father. I wanted to talk about the blood. The meat.

"Doesn't, not don't," I said. "Or actually: does not. Say does not."

"I wish Dad were here," my son said.

"I do too. But we must persevere."

I uncrossed my legs & leaned toward him. "If you're having problems at school I want you to know that you can tell me. You can trust me. Actually. No. You must tell me." I remembered the word imperative. "It is imperative."

Then I remembered something someone said once in a movie: "No matter what problems you may be having, I love you very much & I will never judge you & nothing will ever change that."

It felt good to say that. I stood up, raised my son to his feet by his hands & hugged him. When I hugged him, I bent my knees so that I was nearly at his eye-level. This conveys respect to a child.

*

That weekend I bought extra-strength detergent. The grocery store had long lines & empty shelves. Even with the new detergent, his white shirts no longer looked truly white.

My son spent the morning playing video games. I sent him outside to get some sun.

At dinnertime I called him in. Sweat had carved odd rivulets through the dust on his forehead. I did not make him wash up. I wanted to watch him filthy. I wanted to watch him eat.

He did not put his napkin on his lap. He did not pause for grace as we did when his father was home. He speared the pork chop with a fork & raised it to his face, biting chunks off. Meat bits & spittle fell from his open mouth. He ate a few bites of the rice, which I'd soaked in butter. He pushed the broccoli aside without pretending to eat it.

When he finished his pork chop, I gave him the one I'd cooked in honor of his father. When he ate that one, I gave him mine. His sweating face flushed pink with the effort of eating.

When done, he drank milk in deep gulps, coming up for air only to ask for more. On the news on the TV the fires were spreading. I looked at the screen & imagined I smelled smoke. The power flickered. The fridge reset itself, then resumed its drone.

*

On Monday fewer cars dropped children off at school. The fires had advanced. Black smoke lined the horizon.

I waved at Mrs. Rabin dropping off Tracy, Mrs. McEwan dropping off Malcolm, & Mrs. Barrett dropping off Tommy. Tommy always wore a ratty bathrobe for some reason. In the morning light, Tommy looked vulnerable. Defenseless.

I stopped at the curb & killed the engine. "OK. The small knife is in your pocket. The big knife is in your bag, inside the hollowed-out math book."

"I know, Mom," my son said, rolling his eyes & looking at the school doors.

He did not want his friends to see us talking. I knew this. I tried to be quick.

"One more moment. Focus. Do this for me," I said.

He faced back, resentful but resigned.

"In case of emergency," I asked, "where do you look?"

He sighed. "Fence line behind the tree."

"Which tree?"

"The weird one with broken limbs."

"Wonderful!"

Some days I am so proud of my son. I leaned in to hug him, but he straight-armed me back. "Not here, Mom. Geez!"

The tightness in my throat made my voice a bit off. "Mommy loves you. Mommy loves you so, so much."

"I know," he said, very quietly, staring out his window.

"Okay, get in there." He scrambled out.

I pushed the button to roll the passenger window down. I was going to yell "Be strong," but the other children were watching, so I stayed silent. The air smelled faintly of burning plastic.

I drove to the neighborhood beyond the school, where thick oak trees muted the outside world. I looked at the houses & thought of their selling prices. I parked, got out, & slung the reusable grocery bag over my shoulder. I wished I'd brought a sweater.

The Gardners' house had no lights, no car in the driveway, so I cut behind it & to the creek. My boots slurped in the wet mud. I remembered my husband laughing when I bought hiking boots. "The only hiking you do is through the mall," he'd said.

I saw a squirrel on the ground. "Look at me now," I told the squirrel. The blood on its nose told me it was dead. Its belly was bloated, but it looked fresh. Another lay a few yards away.

At the fence line I saw Mrs. Rabin a few hundred feet off, kneeling at the dirt. I waved. She waved back, but it was only a small wave, from the elbow. I walked away from my son's & my planned spot, but I kept her in sight. She stood & walked into the trees without waving goodbye. Dirt smudged her jeans. She was also wearing hiking boots.

After burying the ball peen hammer & another knife, I walked to where Mrs. Rabin had been kneeling. A signpost just through the fence read "Drug Free Zone." A good visual marker, but maybe too obvious. The dirt was still loose. I dug up her plastic bag easily.

*

I sat in the car with the radio on. The news full of static. Fires. Fires. Fires.

A layer of ash had settled over the storage center & the parking lot, like dust in a long-undisturbed attic. My tire tracks were the only lines in the ash. The sun swelled behind the haze.

The brass padlock was still shiny. At first I came here every day. But with the school situation I hadn't visited since last week. I stepped in & flicked the light switch.

Furniture wrapped in old sheets lined one wall. White cardboard boxes stacked up against the other, each labeled in thick black pen in my handwriting. The smell had worsened.

My husband's body had grown more balloon-like, but I could still see him inside what he'd become. Sagging black skin folded over the duct tape that bound him to the dining chair. Fuzzy fungus bloomed from his open mouth. His throat had swollen so much it had torn around the rope. A black halo of stains pooled beneath the chair.

I circled my husband, careful not to step in the muck. I knelt beside him & looked into his misshapen face. His open eyes had dried & split.

"Oh," I said. "Oh darling. I don't know what to do. I just don't know what to do."

TRAIN

You are on a train. Rain washes against the train windows in sheets, warping & obscuring what is outside the train so that one moment it looks like you are riding through a dense & verdant forest & the next moment it looks like you are riding through a devastated city & the next moment it looks like you are on a tall bridge, over a river so far below you it is impossible to see. On the bridge, your train slows. Another train passes in the other direction, also moving slowly. From each window a face stares at you. Each face expressionless. Each face the same face. You touch your fingers to your face to make sure your face is still there. The train speeds up again, into a tunnel of trees. This is the oldest forest on Earth, trees cultivated for centuries to form this tunnel. The trees over the centuries, finding themselves wanting to form this tunnel, helping each other, making space for the smaller trees, opening branches to let sunlight down to lower trees. The train's light throws the gnarled branches into weird reliefs, Art Deco mosaics of cracked & fissured bark, rococo leaves, chiaroscuro, as if the trees had found the path through the heart of the natural & into art. The train emerges from the tunnel of trees & stops at a train station. The train is taking a break here, exhausted after the tunnel of trees. You disembark with the other passengers. The train station is filled with hundreds of doors. Above each door, a bronze plaque, patinated & aged, spells out a name. Each passenger has a door with their name painted onto it. You find the door with your name & open it & walk through. Your door opens into a vast garden, filled with plants & flowers of the most elaborate beauty, each a color no human has ever seen before. In the center of the garden sits a tall tank of water. Inside the tank, a bronze mermaid swims in slow circles, singing a wordless, lilting song. You sit on a stone bench beside the tank. The bronze mermaid swims to you. She sings for you & so the song is for you. The song slips into you & fills you. You feel the song in the tips of your fingers, in the hairs on your wrist. You open your mouth & sing in harmony with the bronze mermaid, two voices joining like river water. Then the conductor shouts *All aboard!* & the mermaid swims away & you return to the train. The train doors close. The train chugs back into motion. There is a smell in the train. A smell you cannot identify. Something pleasant. Something that almost makes you recall a moment in your childhood with a friend you had otherwise forgotten about. You check your phone & that childhood friend is in your contacts. You call them & describe the smell as best you can, thinking they might be able to identify—through the shared memory—what the smell is a smell of. As you talk, your childhood friend says, *I'm sorry, but you're breaking up. I'm sorry, all your words are coming out like dust. I'm sorry but the river has no heart.* You keep talking, keep describing the smell. It doesn't matter if your childhood friend can hear you or not. That's not the point. That's not the point at all. There is a costume party taking place in your traincar. You are dressed like a derailed train. Everyone else is dressed at witches or scarecrows or tin men or Dorothy. *I didn't know this was a Wizard of Oz-themed party*, you say to a person dressed as a flying monkey. *It's not*, she says. *What is your costume?* she says. *I'm a witch*, you say. Back in your seat, you watch out the window as buildings pass. As the train moves forward, the buildings change from sleek modern skyscrapers to boxy steel structures to huge behemoths of raw stone to four-story buildings of red brick to wooden houses to shacks to huts. The train is moving backward through the history of cities. The huts lead to trees, then ferns, & then the train has progressed to a time before plants, & where is this city even located at this point, hundreds of millions of years in the past, in flux of the Pangaeic land mass? Where are you on this planet? Nothing is stable. Nothing remains still. Then you see your friend's house & you're so excited to see it that you try to take a picture of the house to send to your friend, but by the time you have your phone ready, the house is way behind you, so you take a photo of your own face & text it to your friend. *Are you OK?* your friend texts back. *I'm just happy to be here*, you text back. You have a small, sentient train as a pet. You keep the train in your pocket. Your pet train wears a bright yellow vest that reads *SERVITS NANINAL*. The train is about four inches tall & very snuggly. You hold your pet train in the crook of your arm. You open a ziploc bag of coal & pinch out a bit of coal & feed it into the train's open mouth. A bright fire burns in the train's mouth. A little kid across the aisle asks if they can pet the train. *Choooooo! Chooooo!* the train says, as the child gently pets with their fingertips. Your pet train spews out a thin tendril of black smoke from its smokestack. *Your train is so cute*, the child says. *I know. We don't deserve trains*, you say to the child. *I dream of trains*, the child says & something ripples in being, as if a train had passed by, shaking all of being to its foundations. There is a recording studio on the train, just past the cafe car & you walk down to see what's poppin' in the studio. En route, you pass through a train car in which a model train set has been set up. The model train circles on a small track, surrounded by tiny models of modest houses, roofs coated with fake snow. Muffled beats rise from the studio. You open the door to the studio. Missy Elliott is inside, sitting at the recording console. Her back is to you. Her fingers slide things, press things, adjust things, twist things. The music, through her adjustments, grows constantly more precise, more correct, like waves of light focusing into a laser. No matter how you move, Missy Elliott's back faces you. You shift this way & that, only to see her back & her back & her back. She is so intent on the process of recording, so inside her own art that everything outside deflects away from her. *Like a diamond*, you say out loud to no one. Then, because you're embarrassed you said that out loud you say *Like an ant*. You have to pee so bad. You rush to the restroom, only to find hundreds of people crowded outside the sliding door. *The alligators are back*, a man says as he dances side to side, hands grasping his groin. Everyone looks to you expectantly. You slide the metal door open & inside dozens of alligators are packed into the restroom floor, all flailing & tailing & baring their teeth. You rush back to the studio with a net & you capture a bit of Missy Elliott's song & return to the restroom. You fling the song to the alligators. The alligators are so interested in the song that they are no longer dangerous. You step gently on their scaly backs to the restroom & adjust your pants & pee. A conductor takes you to the back of the train. *This is where we keep the ocean*, she says. She opens a door & the wind whips your hair & clothes against you. The train is riding through a vast desert. Behind the traincars, the train pulls dozens of huge glass-walled aquariums, miles of aquarium cars. Each aquarium carries an enormous sea animal, blue whales, giant squid, kraken, behemoths, all splashing contentedly in their tanks of seawater. You climb onto the top of the train as it speeds through mountains. To your left, a river of clear water twists & spills downhill through the canyon. To your right, steep stone walls rise up to hills filled with trees ablaze with autumn colors. You walk along the top of the train. Glass skylights are set into the train's roof. Looking down the skylights into the train you see sleeping people having terrible dreams. In one a guy is at a conference but only wearing red silky underwear. He runs around trying to cover himself up as his peers ask him detailed questions that he must, out of professional courtesy, answer in depth. In another, a woman finds out her father, whom she thought dead for many decades, whom she always thought a good guy, has been alive all this time & just didn't want to see her. In another, a tidal wave is approaching, & the dreamer cannot escape. You bang on the skylight. *It's just a dream!* you shout. *You can breathe underwater!* The dreamer looks up at you. Understanding fills their face. They hold their breath & plug their nose as the tidal wave crashes over them. When it has passed they rise out of the water & take a deep breath as if it were their first breath. The train enters a city. It slows but doesn't stop, rolls through the train station made of mirrors. You are reflected in every surface, thousands of yous staring back. And then, just as quickly, the train exits the station & plunges into an unlit tunnel & you are inside the train again, at your seat. In the darkness the window reflects your image back to you. The image looks just like you, but you suspect it might be someone else's reflection. You walk up the train, moving from car to car to the front car. The conductor opens the door & invites you in. You sit & look out the small round window. Thousands of kites fly in the air before the train, strings taut, the kites pulling the train forward. *Kite-powered*, the conductor says. *Want to try?* The conductor's hands are wrapped with thousands of strings. You slide your hands into the loops & gather the kites in your hands. You feel the power of the wind in the kites. You feel the kites clinging to the breath of the earth. You twist your hands this way & that, positioning each kite individually, better situating each to the wind. It is delicate work, but you are innately skilled at it—you were born for this. With a twitch, you turn two kites into the wind & they pull harder, the train speeding up. With another slight adjustment, four kites flatten against the breeze. You pull the train up the canyon. You return the kites to the conductor. Dizzy Gillespie is in your traincar. People gather around him. He puts his finger in his mouth & blows & his cheeks puff out like balloons. When he stops everyone is like *Do it again! Do it again!* You put your finger in your mouth & blow, trying to make your cheeks big. You blow & you blow, until there is a popping noise. You've popped one of your cheeks. You don't want anyone else to see that you've popped your cheek. You hold the pieces of your broken cheek closed with one hand & return to your seat. Outside the train it is snowing heavily. You push your cheek against the cold window & keep it pressed there until it goes numb. Abandoned factories & towering landfills & burning hospitals slip by. When you look back inside, you are the only person on this train. *Hello?* you say, though you are alone. You walk down the aisle of the moving train, touching seat-tops for balance. You press the button to open the doors between trains. You enter another empty train car. You walk through this one & into the next train car. Also empty. The next is empty & the next & the next. You walk through so many empty train cars that you wonder how long a train could be. You press the button & the doors slide open & you enter another train car. Someone is sitting in one of the seats. She looks up at you, eyes wide. You stop. Shocked to see another person after so much emptiness. She looks away from you. The door behind you slides shut. You sit in a seat far away from the other person. You squeeze up against the window. You stare out at a passing suburb, identical houses decaying in identical ways. After a minute or so, the other person gets up & walks down the aisle & sits beside you. She looks over your shoulder, out the window. The two of you watch the ruined world, in silence, but together. After a bit, you return to your traincar. There is a small volcano on the far end. Everyone pretends not to notice it. People quietly move away when lava courses from the volcano's tip, not looking up from their phones. The conductor enters the car. He is going to check tickets. No one has purchased a ticket. Everyone gets up & forms a line in front of you, wanting to buy tickets from you. You don't have any tickets, but you don't want to disappoint the people in line. They've waited so patiently. You get a pad of paper out & write

TRAIN TICKET – TODAY– $15. You take cash from each person in line & stuff it into an envelope. You write *TICKET MONEY* on the envelope & slip it inside a book in your bag. The conductor scans each person's ticket. After each scan, the doohickey beeps & the conductor smiles & says *Welcome to your train*. You open a water bottle & lift it to your lips. A man across the aisle says, in a gruff & serrated voice, *You open a water bottle & lift it to your lips*. You turn to the man. The man says, *You turn to the man. Stop*, you say. *You say Stop*, he says. You stand up & gather your belongings. *You stand up & gather your belongings*, he says. You head down the aisle. *You head down the aisle*, he says. You turn back. *You turn back*, he says. *You are an untrustworthy narrator*, you say. The man grows still, inward-looking. *One should never have to meet one's narrator*, he says, his voice so quiet you can barely hear it over the grind & rumble of the train. You step into the next train car. Each seat is occupied by one of your birthdays. All your birthdays are asleep. You step carefully, not wanting to wake your birthdays. If you can make it through without waking them, you will make it through the day without growing a year older. You step into the next traincar to find it full of gravel & trash & thorny scrubby bushes. There is a rustling in the bushes beyond the train tracks. A small person emerges; it's impossible to gauge her age. She walks up to you. She bends over & picks a shard of glass from the pile of broken bottles. She takes the shard of glass & runs it down her arm, slicing the skin open. Beneath her skin, something glows, cool & bioluminescently green. *This is the price of admission*, she says. She hands you the shard of glass. *You have to let the light out*, she says, *or it will destroy you from within*. You press the sharp point of the glass to your arm & slide it down. Nothing happens. Your skin will not open. You try again. Nothing. *It's too late*, she says. *Look*. She points out the window. The sun is rising over distant mountains. *It's already here*, she says. As you look out the window. There is a voice-over in a foreign language. You understand what is being said, though you don't know the language. A child sits beside you. *This is my indoor voice*, she says & opens her hands to reveal a large, dark green toad. The toad looks at you placidly. *What is your indoor voice?* she says. *Your indoor voice is this train.* Police walk up & down the aisles of the train, looking for a bank robber. The police walk right by you. Your arms are full of white sacks stuffed with stolen money. The police move to another car. The train plunges into a tunnel, travels deep into the earth, the darkness outside the windows grows darker, darker, tangibly dark. The train twists around tight curves, bounces over bumps, spins circles & doubles back the way it came from. *The driver must be lost*, you think. You make your way to the front of the train. Between cars there are no walls & you are surrounded by the tangible dark. You gather the darkness with your hands & fill your pockets with it. You continue moving forward. You reach the driver, sitting before a small round window. A thin beam of wan light barely interrupts the dark before him. *Are you lost?* you say. The train dips down a great hill in the dark. *No*, the driver says. *I'm just following the directions.* He holds up a stack of paper more than a foot thick. *The problem is that the directions never end. When they built this track they failed to build a destination.* The train is the future. You are riding the future through the darkness without end. This train is your life, from birth to death. Your life is the size & shape of a train. Your life is the size & shape of the future. Your whole life is a movement through the dark. You are shopping for a mattress. You are crying in a hospital. You hold someone's hand until your palms sweat. You stand on a riverbank. You watch a passing train. It is the train of your life. You can feel the weight of the passing train in your bones. The train is endless. A hawk launches from a nearby tree, startling you. Someone touches your cheek. That hand in your hand. The lull of the river over rocks. You are spinning in the scent of sunlight. You are singing & others are singing & the songs become one song. There is an echo in the sunlight. The hand in your hand. The ringing song of the river;

the song grows stronger, denser, a chorus of singers, one by one, joining in the singing. You join in the singing. You sing until there is no difference between your voice & the river's voice. The final traincar passes & the train is gone.

THE MAN WHO MARRIED A HOUSE

There was a man who married a house. He lived in a neighborhood of suburban two-story houses, mostly built in the forties. Trees leaned over the roads. There were no sidewalks. When people walked their dogs or put their athletic clothing on to walk or jog they did these things in the road. Sometimes they would wave at cars as they passed, but more often they did not.

The man did not love his house, not in the way that a human can love a human. It was a marriage of convenience, of ease. The wedding, of course, was held at home.

His mother thought the house was wonderful, as did his best friend & his two sisters. While they all found it unorthodox, they gave the marriage their blessings. The only one who did not give his blessing was the man's brother. "I do not think this is a house," the brother said. "I think this is a woman pretending to be a house."

The brother's objections were disregarded. At the ceremony there was an open bar & OK food, bad music. The sound system boomed music through the neighborhood & neighbors turned their TVs up. The first dance between the man & the house was a bit awkward, but everyone pretended it was not.

The brother left soon after the ceremony. He did not have

a single drink & did not even talk to the bridesmaid with whom he'd been paired to walk down the aisle.

The gifts for the new couple included the usual furnishings & cookware, but also included a gift certificate for the buffing of hardwood floors & a semi-erotic tapestry.

The brother & the man did not talk after the wedding. They did not talk for three years. In this time the man & the house had two children: a girl & a small house. The man & the house had all the trappings of a successful marriage, but the man began to regret his decision. He did not love the house & he began to wonder what a marriage to a woman would be like. Or perhaps he wondered what it was like to be married to someone you love.

The man had never been in love. He claimed that he didn't believe in love. Love is just a biological function to get humans to do unnatural things, like care for others, give up one's own supplies. When the idea of love came up in conversation with friends he would rant about this & his friends would mock him, all in good fun. He claimed he'd married rationally, rather than emotionally. He said this as a point of pride. The rational is better than the emotional.

Then one day the man walked into the bathroom & saw the house emerging from the shower. On the floor of the bathroom sat pieces of house. The room was foggy with steam. She was drying her hair & the towel covered her face, but she must have felt the draft because she lowered the towel & looked at the man.

The woman was bright pink from the heat. Bright pink of skin. She had breasts & pubic hair & hips.

At the moment the man realized that his brother had been right. That he'd been deceived into marrying a house by a woman disguised as a house.

The man got into his car & drove away. He drove until he was falling asleep at the wheel & then he pulled off the highway & checked into a motel. All the cars around him had Ohio license plates, so he guessed he was in Ohio.

The next morning he went to Denny's & ate breakfast & went back to the hotel. His phone had calls from the house & one from his mom. He dialed his brother, whom he hadn't talked to in years.

"Hey," his brother said.

"Hey," the man said.

There was a pause. The man considered hanging up.

"So... you were right," the man said. Then he told his brother what he'd seen in the bathroom. The bright pink of the skin of the belly. The discarded house pieces on the ground.

The brother was quiet. "You should come here. Stay here for a few days. We need to talk."

That night the man pulled up the dirt driveway into his brother's land, out in the hills, past the End State Maintenance signs. The man had never understood how his brother could live so far out from civilization, so far from the grocery stores that stay open all night & the shops filled with everything. The lights were on, though it was almost midnight. The dogs barked like a circus.

The man got out & walked up to the door. His brother was inside, holding one dog's collar with each hand as the man walked in. The dogs pulled toward the man, wanting to jump up on him & lick his face.

"Need a water? Beer?" the brother asked as he pulled the eager dogs into the bedroom & closed the door on them.

"Beer," the man said.

The brother opened the fridge & retrieved two bottles. He handed one over, unscrewed the top of his own & leaned against the kitchen counter.

"Go ahead," the man said.

"Go ahead what?"

"Go ahead & tell me you told me so," the man said.

The brother laughed. "It's not like that. Not like that at all."

Both of them drank their beers. The man looked around. Some things had changed since he'd been here last, but most things were the same. Same table. Same clean everything.

"What's it like then if it's not like that?" the man asked.

"It's hard to explain," the brother said. "I think I might just have to show you this."

The brother put his beer down on the clean counter & un-buttoned the front of his shirt.

"What the fuck," the man said, laughing.

The brother pulled the sides of his shirt apart. There in the middle of his chest, among curls of dark chest hair, was a small door. The brother averted his eyes. He stood there, holding his shirt open. Waiting.

The man could smell something like fresh wood.

"Go ahead," the brother told the man, "open it."

The man looked at the small door for a bit. He finished his beer & put the empty bottle on the table behind him. Then the man knelt on one knee in front of his brother. There was still red irritation where the door jambs were affixed into this brother's chest. This must have been a recent renovation. He grabbed the tiny handle between his thumb & forefinger. The handle was body-warm.

The man turned the handle. With a small click, the door in his brother's chest opened.

MY ARM & ME

Ellen & 'lil-Ellen & I were cleaning up the house. It had been a wet winter & the basement had gone musty. Since the weather turned warm, one by one, each neighbor on the block had hauled batches of black plastic bags to the curb. Ellen decided it was our turn.

I kept the box that contained my arm in the closet next to the front door, with the lawn games, the old winter coats, so that closet was my duty. I had everything out on the floor: puffy down coats, a jacket that had once been white, a dart board from my college days, bags of mittens & pilled scarves. I stacked a croquet set in a dissolving cardboard box atop of Nerf lawn darts in an unopened box. So much crap can fit into one closet.

"Trash it," Ellen said. "Trash it all!" It seemed drastic but I didn't argue.

Lil-Ellen walked up to the pile & without saying a word pulled two jackets out. She walked up the stairs to her bedroom on the third floor.

I got the box of trash bags from the kitchen, & Ellen & I began stuffing everything into one. Once or twice I considered keeping one of these old coats, in case I ever took up skiing or snowshoeing. But Ellen was right, we hadn't worn these things in years, decades.

She held the bags open & I picked up one coat at a time, wedging them into the bag, my one arm sinking deep into the softness. We ended up with three plump black plastic bags, as distended as tumors.

The only thing I hadn't taken out of the closet was the box containing my severed arm. After my arm got cut off, I bought a nice glass display box for it. I stored that box inside another cardboard box so it wouldn't get scratched or shattered. The glass box was sealed. It didn't smell or anything. Despite getting this nice display box for my arm, I'd never hung it up on the walls.

The box containing the box containing my arm looked wrong in the empty closet. Isolated, lonely.

*

I hung my arm over the mantle, & in the following days there was more silence around the house. I knew Ellen wouldn't like it & she didn't. Lil-Ellen, if she noticed, expressed her reaction through her usual quietude & her usual rolling of eyes. Perhaps there was a deeper quiet to her, a more fervent rolling of the eyes. But perhaps not?

The arm was pale brown, my skin tone in winter. I'd cleaned the glass display box with Windex. Measured & perfectly placed it above the mantle. On the mantle sat photos of me & Ellen holding the tiny newborn 'lil-Ellen, my folks, her folks, a few other people.

I explained to Ellen repeatedly that it wasn't a joke, my arm over the mantle. It made me feel good to have the arm there. But even I admit, it was not beautiful.

*

One time, long before I'd lost my arm, before lil-Ellen was born, Ellen & I had borrowed a boat from a friend & were on a big lake in Wisconsin. We found an island in the middle of the lake. We could barely see the coastline from the island.

"Wouldn't it be wonderful to live here?" I asked Ellen. "To disappear & build our own house & gather food from the woods?"

Ellen looked at the sun in the sky & the deep green canopy of trees above her. "Can we" she asked "eat the boaters who come to visit the island on weekends?"

"We'll need to." I said. "We'll have to protect our land."

We dug a pit & built a fire. We gathered wood from the trees & logs to sit upon. There was a blackberry bush & I came back with my hat full of blackberries. I was frightened by the immensity of our decision, but I also felt like I'd stepped into the universe I'd been born in, after a lifetime away.

After we had sex in the grass, we laid naked in the sun. Ellen's eyes were closed. I got between her legs. She arched her back. The grass tickled my bare skin.

I was woken up by Ellen throwing my clothes onto me. "C'mon, she said, it's getting dark. Never be able to find their dock in the dark."

"Sure" I said & stretched. My neck felt weird from the ground.

We got into the boat & I rowed back toward what I thought was their house. By the time we got there it was well after dark. Our friends had put four huge lanterns onto the dock to guide us.

*

It's difficult to notice changes in things you see every day. You never think of how much your hair has grown on any one day, just one day you need a haircut. But, the color of the arm had changed. It was looking more like flesh.

I didn't say anything to Ellen, & if she noticed she didn't say anything to me. But she had begun to spend more time in the living room. She used to read in bed, now she read on the couch. I'd pour her a cup of coffee in the morning & she'd take it in there.

*

I was in the basement when Ellen called me up. I was trying to fix the washing machine, but just dicking around a bit before we inevitably called a pro. Even before I lost the arm I was a mess with tools, & since then I can't do much. But I do try to keep from getting cynical.

"What is that?" she asked, sounding displeased.

She was pointing at the arm. "That's my arm," I said.

"Shut up, I mean this."

I got up close & looked. There was something coming out of the arm, where it would meet the socket if it were still on my body. It did not look like mold. It looked like a bubble.

"Don't know," I said.

"Is that normal?" she asked.

"I have no idea. We've had it in the closet for years," I said. "Maybe it does this."

"It looks weird," she said & looked at me.

"Yep," I said. "It sure does."

We looked at it for about ten more minutes. We hypothesized.

*

We ate in the living room, with the arm. Ellen had some big project at work that she was preparing at home. She'd spread the papers over the kitchen table. She'd never done that before. One day she moved us all into the living room.

It was nice to eat in the living room. It felt like a vacation. No TV on, so we talked. Even 'lil-Ellen said a few words, even laughed when I'd made the baby carrots dance like little ballerina feet.

The bubble on my arm expanded. It pressed against the glass case.

After one dinner lil-Ellen looked at the arm. We had been guessing about what was causing the bubble. It had become something of a family game.

"Fuck!" lil-Ellen yelped.

"Ellen Norman!" Ellen said with narrowed eyes. "We do not use that kind..."

"It's a fucking eye!" lil-Ellen yelled.

She was right. An eye.

It was like the eye on a fetal animal inside the womb, pink & mammalian, still sealed shut. The white & dark of the eyeball darted beneath the thin skin.

Ellen grabbed me so hard it felt electric. I knew she'd drawn blood. But I wasn't thinking about that at all. The eye was twitching, alive.

*

Over the next week it grew more & more rapidly.

I shattered the glass case to get the arm out. Broken glass grazed its skin & a line of watery blood formed.

We put the arm on the guest bed. It had grown not like a developing animal but like a body pushing itself out of the arm head-first. Eyes the first day, face the next. The mouth covered by a layer of stretched skin. The parts were all half-formed, like charcoal sketches.

More fingers grew, pulling the end of the arm open wider. The next morning a leg pushed out, then the next another leg.

A day later we covered its developing genitals with an old pair of my boxers. The penis & testicles were vague, like soft dough.

By then the head had begun making noises. Grunts & gasps. Its eyes followed us across the room. Ellen was, she claimed, disgusted, but she checked on it every chance she got. Lil-Ellen took photos, tracking development, scientific in her interest.

After I realized that the face growing on its shoulders was my face, I visited the guest room less often.

*

I looked at it in the mirror: my shoulder, my wound, the spot where my body ended, like a blink. For so long, it was just a fact about my life. Where other people had a mass of muscle

& bone connecting their chest to their left arm, I had these scars.

Ellen came into our bathroom. We made eye contact in the mirror. I suddenly wanted to cover my shoulder up, to put a t-shirt on. The possibility of her looking at my scars, looking at what I did not have, it made me feel ten years old.

"He said my name," she said.

*

It could say her name & 'lil-Ellen's of course. Same name.

It could say book, cup, beer, pen, newspaper. Window, bed, brush, shirt.

Within a few days it had strung words together in stunted English. It asked for things & we got them. Soon it could hold its head from lolling & move its hands toward objects, though the fingers could not grasp.

Every time Ellen entered the room, he followed her with his eyes & head like a puppy. When I entered the room with Ellen, it gave me no notice. But when I went in alone it stared intently, eyes scouring my body, resting on where my arm had been.

I tried to meet its gaze, but it was difficult to look at. It was like me & also like an amphibian. But it did have two arms. That it did.

*

I go to sleep early & she goes to sleep late. So I didn't notice the first night Ellen stayed in the guest room with the Me.

Awake before the alarm, as always, I thought she must have

woken before me. I walked down the stairs but the kitchen was dark. The house quiet with predawn. Walking up to the third floor, I found myself stepping carefully to avoid any creaking floorboards. Quietly, I turned the doorknob & opened the door to the guest room.

She was still wearing the sweats & t-shirt she'd had on last night. She had the covers curled around her sleeping body & she was facing away from the Me. He slept on his back, breathing heavily & noisily, just like I'm told I do.

I closed the door & stepped silently down to the kitchen. I started the coffee & put some bread in the toaster. I turned the radio on.

She wasn't in his arms. She still had her clothes on. That was something. It was OK.

*

The Me was up & walking. I came home from work to find him on the couch with his feet up, wearing my comfy t-shirt, reading a book I'd had on the shelf for years, one I'd always meant to get to.

Since he was on the couch, I went outside & mowed the lawn. Later, he was in the bedroom looking through the closets, so I went to the basement & sorted the laundry. I tidied the house, avoiding the room he was in. Being in the same room made me feel like an old photograph of myself.

The house was cleaner than it had ever been. I was starting to get better with tools, finding any excuse to use them. Ellen & 'lil-Ellen talked more.

If he noticed my presence, it was only to stare. He looked at my face & touched his own. Looked at my gut & rubbed his hands over his smaller belly. When he looked at the space where my arm was not & touched his arm, my arm, he turned his head away from me & looked at his arm. He ran his other hand up & down the arm. Stroking it.

*

When Ellen & I were first dating she used to love to play newlyweds. "Carry me over the threshold, my darling," she'd say in a 1940s Hollywood voice. I'd pick her up, cradle her in my arms, & walk into the library or the thrift store or wherever.

I loved the surprise of how easy it was to pick her up each time. She hated to be thrown over my shoulder, which I thought was hilarious. We'd walk in the woods & I'd pick her up & toss her over my shoulder like a sack of potatoes. She'd struggle, but she'd laugh. Often, we'd end up with pants around our ankles, her legs wrapped around my waist.

After my arm got cut off, after it all healed, I could still pick her up. We did it a few times. She had to lean into me just so. We had to really try. It was work. Eventually we stopped.

*

The guest bed was not above our bedroom, but I could hear the noises. After two weeks of sleeping in the bed alone, I waited until the Me & Ellen were on one of their walks. I moved some of my clothes into the guest room. I moved the clothes of mine that he had claimed down into the bedroom. I took back my Brooks Brothers shirt. It's my favorite shirt.

At dinner one night he asked 'lil-Ellen how her day was. When she rolled her eyes at him I hid my smirk, pleased to see him rebuked as I would be. But then he held her hand between his two hands, looked into her face & said "I understand your resistance, I do. I know this is a crazy world. Often truly awful. None of us will ever understand it. None of us chose to be born. But since we are here, you & me, & I love you, I'd really like to know what your days are like, what your life is like." She sat still for a few moments. Her hand in his soft grip. And then she told him things.

I never knew how much she cared about that clarinet in the battered black case. Whenever I saw her play I could only watch her fingers slip up & down the metal keys. There was something comforting in the dexterity of her motion. I never knew how much stress 'lil-Ellen felt.

As she opened up to the Me, told more & more about her life, her feelings, her experiences, I realized this girl with whom I'd shared an entire life was somehow empty to me, a cicada skin on a screen door, a plastic mask a grocery store sells at Halloween.

COMEDY

Comedy lined up the bodies on his work table. Cut a slit around the neck of the first, then another slit down the belly. Rolled the skin off, revealing the brown-red patchwork of muscles.

He cut the second & peeled back the skin. He dropped it in the box with the first. Then the third. Then the fourth.

Inside the house, glass things shattered. Solid things cracked.

He cut the fifth body. As he peeled the skin back, long white worms wriggled into the air, then sucked back into the body. He grabbed one slow worm between finger & thumb. It bit him. He let go. It vanished back into the skinned body.

He filled a white bucket with water from the metal sink.

Inside the house something thumped. Then a shattering. Someone screamed. Or maybe it was wailing.

He dropped the worm-filled body into the bucket & pushed it under the water with a stick. He fixed the stick so it held the body down.

He smelled smoke. From inside the house.

He picked up the first body, slit open the stomach, & pulled the guts & organs out. He dropped the body back into the box. He did this with the second, third & fourth. A blue layer of smoke filled the garage.

In the bucket, dozens of white worms wriggled frantically along the top of the water. He fished them out with a small net & poured them into a white plastic margarine container.

Comedy cut three thin slits across the palm of his right hand. Bright red blood slid out of the wounds. He pushed his hand into the plastic container of worms. The tips of the worms blindly nudged at the cuts. First a nibble. Then a bite. And then the first worm slipped in.

MY FATHER IS A DISAPPEARANCE

I see him from the corner of my eye, drinking a cup of coffee at the kitchen table, watching the MacNeil Lehrer News Report. By the time I turn back, he's gone, & the TV continues to speak about soldiers in Kuwait & Scud Missiles.

The last time we talked was months ago. I was mowing the lawn, listening to Aerosmith on my walkman. I saw him cutting a dead branch from the dogwood. I hadn't seen him in days. I ran over.

"Dad!" I said. "How are you?" I was sweaty. It was hot & humid. I didn't know how to ask anything better. I pulled my headphones off as I ran & they hung on the back of my neck.

"Oh, the feathers & the bones," he mumbled. "The feathers, the feathers & the bones." Or maybe it was something else. I'd left the lawnmower running.

Someone across the street started a car & I turned. When I looked back the branch cutters sat on the bare patch beneath the tree & my father was gone.

Since then, I see him maybe once a week. Sometimes reading a book in bed. Once beside the unlit fireplace. The toilet flushes but no one emerges from the bathroom.

Once, I tried to keep him in my sights & stared as I approached, but something blurry happened & as I neared him he was gone. I stood in the room & looked around, sniffing to maybe catch some smell of him, though he never really had a smell. Then I found something else to do.

I asked my mom but she said "Oh, you know your dad," as if that were an answer & continued her crossword puzzle.

My one brother acts like he doesn't care. "Fuck him," he said, legs sticking out from under the Mustang.

My other brother didn't know what I was talking about. "He's in the living room right now," he said, half-laughing, but also giving me a look like "You OK, weirdo?"

I checked the living room, but it was empty, an open book about Vietnam on the easy chair. I returned to my brother's room to tell him our father was gone but my older brother was gone now too.

I asked my third brother when the last time he'd seen our father was. He was playing with He-Mans. "I dunno what you mean," he said.

"Our dad? You know, dad?" I asked, putting a hand over the green-skinned action figure.

"I don't know who you're talking about," he said & pulled the He-Man from my grip.

I do feel like a weirdo. Always searching the house for him. Looking through shoe boxes of photographs. I see traces of him: keys for the Saab on the dining room table, Newsweek in the bathroom, a box of Frosted Mini-Wheats open on the table. I hear his voice in the kitchen but when I run in I find only a steaming, half-empty bowl of soup on the table, with the spoon sticking out at four o'clock. I sit down & lift the spoon to my lips. The tomato soup sweet & salty. I keep the spoon in my mouth & close my eyes until I taste its metal.

My mom walks in. "What the hell are you doing?" she said.

"Nothing." I drop the spoon onto the table with a clink.

"That was supposed to be dinner." She sighs as she opens the cabinet.

This morning, the floor creaks as I brush my teeth. He is looking at me. His eyes bloodshot & his tie wrinkled. He has something in his hands. A pad of paper & his fancy fountain pen. He is offering the pad of paper to me. I bend to spit, & when I raise my head he is gone. I pick the pad off the hardwood floor. The only thing written there, right at the top of the first page, is *MY STORY*. The rest of the paper is blank.

THE PHOTOGRAPHER
& THE VERY TALL MAN

The sunset was lovely. The photographer looked at it through his camera, then without his camera, trying to decide which view was more lovely. The black foothills in the foreground were framed by distant snow-covered mountains, which in turn were framed by the pink & golden clouds. A perfect calendar photo.

The photographer climbed the hill for a better vantage. He reached the top just as the sun dropped behind the mountains. In the fading light, the path he'd followed disappeared. He'd have to sleep beneath the stars.

He spread his jacket over a patch of grass & lay down. Pulling his arms inside his sweater, he tucked his hands into the waistband of his jeans. He thought about the man's body he'd found last month, yellow & dried, hanging from the noose. The high desert air had sucked the moisture from it, like the mummies he'd seen in Mexico, mouth gaping, dried eyeballs fallen from the sockets like two old dates. The body had swung lightly in the breeze.

As the temp dropped, he wrapped the jacket around himself & zipped up. When he inhaled, the air seemed to stop against his thick tongue & lodge there. He tried to think about women he'd loved, sweat on their throats, the warm weight in the dark. But it was growing too cold. And the hanged man's desiccated fingers kept intruding, twisted in arthritic contortions.

The photographer sat up to adjust his jacket. In the direction he'd come from, he spotted a faint yellow light. Through the zoom lens, he saw a window & the outline of a shack. Rising, he fumbled his way down the hill.

When the photographer reached the shack, he called out hello, but got no answer.

The shack was made of corrugated tin, propped up with cinder blocks & sewn together with wire. It had a wooden door.

He knocked, but no response. He pressed his ear to the door. Silence. He opened it.

Inside, a very tall man sat crouched on a red milk crate beside an electric lantern, reading a book.

The very tall man turned his head to the photographer. The photographer greeted him in English. The man shook his head. He responded in a language that sounded Russian, but the photographer shook his head. The photographer tried Italian & Spanish but the man only shook his head & smiled. The very tall man tried another language, unfamiliar as well. The man threw his hands up, palms raised, & laughed. The photographer laughed too.

The photographer's stomach tightened painfully. He mimed food, but the tall man shook his head. The photographer mimed drink, but again he shook his head. The photographer sighed, like an actor. He pulled out his camera, absent-mindedly, & glanced through the viewfinder, adjusted for low light. He took a few pictures: the pile of old quilts in one corner, a blue milk crate full of cracked plates & tea cups, the very tall man's knees bent up past his chin.

The hike had left the photographer exhausted. He tried to remember his last real meal, but his memory blurred. Yesterday? The day before? The thought of food tightened his stomach more painfully. He gasped & doubled over, seizing his abdomen.

The very tall man looked at the photographer & nodded. He raised finger & stood up. His knees & ankles crackled. At full height he'd have pushed through the roof of the shack. Instead, he crouched, back hunched & rounded.

He returned with a child's cowboy hat, made of faded purple felt, & a knife. He slit the knife across his wrist until blood welled. He winced, then smiled wanly. The blood flowed into the hat. He stretched his hand back to keep the cut vein open. When the hat was a third full, he pushed it into the photographer's hands.

The photographer held the hat, uncertain. The very tall man wrapped a blue bandana around his wrist & mimed drinking. "Treenk!" he said. He lit a cigarette with a match & licked some blood from his palm, where it dripped past the bandana.

The photographer drank. He got blood on his face. He licked his lips. He wiped blood from his face & licked his fingers.

"See! See!" the very tall man said. He stood, crackling again, & dug through a pile. He pulled out a photo album & presented it. "Pho-toe-gaff," he said & mimed a camera's click.

The photographer again nodded. He set the hat on the dirt floor & opened the photo album. The leather cover was scratched & worn to sandpapery tatters. He thought of the hanged man. When he'd lifted the body to cut it from the rafters, dried skin had sloughed off & powdered his hands.

The first page showed a group of men in rural Russian

clothes, heavy coats & fur hats, standing around a burning pile of bodies. Legs & arms stuck out of the fire at dubious angles. The men raised rifles & torches in celebration.

The very tall man motioned for him to turn the page. The photographer turned the page. The next photo showed a man & a woman in formal dress, holding hands & visibly remaining still. Flames had scorched their hair away. The woman's face was blackened. Fire sprouted from their shoulders. Below the waist, their formal clothes remained intact, their matrimonial pose stoic.

The next page showed a burning mass in a wooden crib. The photograph had been hand-tinted, flames in pink & pastel orange, the room in pale blues.

The photographer turned the image up to the very tall man & lifted his arms in a question's gesture.

The very tall man beamed. "Pho-toe-gaff."

The next photo showed men in suits at a long table, all facing the camera. Three in the center were on fire. One a blur of flailing arms. Another just starting to catch, face composed, staring at the camera with dark eyes. The next a gazebo in flames. Inside, women in wide-skirted dresses burned. Each looked directly into the camera's eye.

The very tall man lit another cigarette. He offered, but the photographer declined. The man took the photo album & turned the pages reverently, until he found what he sought. A young woman. Her legs & half half of her torso burnt away, the rest untouched. The flames had burnt away her clothes or perhaps she'd been nude. One bare breast was flecked with ash. Her face was untouched & pale, eyes open, looking to the camera, both carnal & bored.

"Love! Love!" the very tall man said.

The remaining blood in the hat had congealed. The very tall man scooped it out, & sliced it with the same knife he'd used to cut his wrist. He handed half to the photographer & ate the other half. He built a small fire in a wide metal pot, feeding the fire old papers & branches & pieces of broken furniture. The shack warmed quickly.

The photographer lay beneath old quilts that smelled of animals. The burnt girl's face stayed with him when he closed his eyes. Her pale face, her one breast. He thought of a woman he'd seen his last time in the city.

It had been morning & he sat on the stone steps of a brownstone, drinking coffee from a Styrofoam cup, waiting for a friend who was always late.

The woman wore dirty sweatpants & a purple zip-up jacket. She was an indeterminate age of someone who'd lived rough a long time. Her hair, maybe once blonde, was matted.

She paced the street across from the photographer, oblivious to him. Abruptly, she pulled her sweatpants down, leaned her ass over the wrought iron fence outside a basement dive bar, & pissed. The piss splattered shrill in the morning stillness. As she pulled her sweatpants up she saw the photographer. She scowled.

She crossed the street toward him. She pointed at him & screamed a racial slur that he was the wrong race for.

Without thinking, as a defense, he raised his camera. Pointed at her.

She stopped. In the middle of the street.

She looked at the photographer. For a moment he saw the child she might have been when she was a child. Then she smiled, gums bare. She raised her arms up like a 50s pin-up, arching her back. Her smile pure & happy.

He shot a few pictures. He smiled back. He rose & took photos from one angle. She bent & tilted her face up to him in a perfect semblance of a model's seductive look. He kneeled on one knee for another angler. She unzipped her purple jacket. No shirt. She pulled one loose breast & put the nipple into her mouth.

She posed like that for the photographer & the photographer took her picture.

He took photo after photo, until a car honked, scaring them both. She screamed at the car. The spell broke. The woman walked away, jacket still unzipped.

RED

Something woke me. My brothers were still in their beds, breathing heavily. I sat up. Everything felt mistaken.

Hugging my pillow, I walked out of our bedroom & into the living room. The light was on, but the room empty. TV sounds came from my parent's room, muffled laughter, muffled applause. All as if I was under a quilt. From the bottom of an aquarium, clay skull with a mouth hanging open, leaking a line of bubbles.

The dog's tags jingled behind their bedroom door. I pushed it open. Dad stood over their bed. The sheets were red. Dad's hands were all red. The dog trotted over to me, red on his shaggy white fur. Dad squatted, splashes of red on his shirt, on his face.

"Cant' sleep?" he asked.

I nodded.

"Come on," he said. "Let's get you back to bed." He took my hand, took me to the kitchen. The red got on my hand & on my pillow.

From the cabinet, Dad got my favorite mug, the one with the superhero. He filled it with water from the tap & handed it to me. The handle red. A drop of red dripped from dad & into the water. It whirled pink. I sipped.

"Drink up," my dad said.

I drank up.

He took my hand & walked me to our bedroom. My dad picked me up & put me into bed. He tucked the covers under me. My pillow was red. He leaned over & stroked my face. His fingers slick & red.

"No more bad dreams, OK?" he whispered.

"OK," I whispered back.

He kissed my forehead. Red cooled on my skin.

He closed the door behind him. My brothers' breaths continued, coarse, in the dark.

*

In the morning Mom woke us for church. We put our good clothes on. My brothers sat in the way-back of the station wagon, making faces at approaching cars. I sat beside with the car seat where my little brother drooled on himself. Dad had the radio loud & a man on the radio talked. I could still feel how the red had cooled on my skin in the night. I watched the side of the road & imagined tigers running beside the car.

My invisible friend sat next to me in the car. I held his hand. His hands were red. Red dripped down his face from a hole on the top of his head. He stuck his finger into the hole & wiggled the finger around. When he pulled his finger out, chunks & red covered it. He sniffed at his finger then stuck it in his mouth.

I fell asleep in church with my legs pulled up onto the pew, my mom's jacket as a pillow. My little brother cried & it woke me up. My older brothers slapped at each other, trying not to let Dad notice.

After church we sat at the kitchen table. Mom served eggs & sausage & crescent rolls hot from the oven. The TV was on & the man on the TV talked. We ate while Dad listened to the TV & talked back to the TV. Then he looked at my mom. He started to stand up. He fell onto the table, face first. His forehead hit with a clunk. Mom screamed. My oldest brother stood up so fast his chair tipped & clunked over. Mom pulled Dad to the floor. Mom told my brother to call 911 & my brother got on the phone. Mom was yelling. I remained sitting. My invisible friend used one long fingernail to scratch at the hole in the top of his head, pulling skin away in ragged strips. I couldn't see Dad, but I heard him.

"What am I doing on the floor," Dad said.

The ambulance came & rolled Dad out on a gurney. Mom went with them.

The phone rang & it was my friend Zach & he asked if I wanted to go to a folk festival with his family. My oldest brother was home so I asked him if I could go & he said yes. I got back on the phone & told Zach yes.

Zach's parents pulled into the driveway. As I was leaving the house my oldest brother said "Here" & gave me a roll of dimes & a roll of pennies. I held them. One roll of coins in each fist. I liked how they made my fists heavy.

My invisible friend sat in the back seat between me & Zach. My invisible friend pulled a strip of skin down from the hole in his head, ripped the skin right down his forehead, revealing glistening red beneath.

*

Something had changed in the dark. My invisible friend sat on the side of my bed. My brothers snored. If I were to go into my parents' bedroom Dad would not be there. Dad was in the hospital. I pulled the covers over my face. My breathing sandpapery.

"Mi-Key," my invisible friend whispered.

I shook my head. "That's not my name," I said.

"Mi-Key, Mi-Key," he whispered.

The covers weighted my breath. Surely I would suffocate.

"Mi-Key."

I peeked my head from the covers. The night air icy.

My invisible friend had a long kitchen knife in his hand.

"Look at this," he said. He pinched the tip of his nose & pulled it. The nose stretched out. The lower lids of his eyes pulled forward. The upper lip of his mouth distended. His nose stretched a foot from his face, farther, too far. He pressed the kitchen knife to his face & slit through the outstretched nose.

There was a hole in his face from the upper lip to his eyelids, but no red came out. Light moved inside the hole, like fireflies in the trees.

"Hold still," he said & leaned over me. His knees pressed on my chest, pressed the breath still. He stretched his severed nose between his two hands & snapped it onto my face. The nose was cold & soft & it tingled. I couldn't move. Some other breath, a cold breath, entered me.

*

Dad wore a white cotton gown. All the patients wore the gowns. Wires & tubes dangled from Dad's body. His twin brother sat by the bed. He talked to Dad & Dad laughed weakly & then coughed.

"Don't make me laugh," Dad said.

The hospital was so bright I couldn't imagine anyone sleeping. It must be this bright all night long. The lights as wide as everything & each day, extending forever in every direction. A maze of lights. The kind monsters enter & never leave. To find your way out you need a long string to trail behind you.

My invisible friend had a large spool of thread & wandered the bright halls of the hospital, laying down more & more trails of string. String everywhere. Layers of string covered the shiny floors, making them dull beneath the bright lights.

Dad laughed & then he coughed. He coughed & then was choking up raw meat sounds. Something beeped. Beeping.

"Mike? Mike?" my uncle said. He held his fingers to Dad's neck. I feared he might be choking him. But my uncle was a doctor.

Nurses ran in. Then a doctor.

My uncle pressed his wide hand against my back & walked me out. The hallways were filled with thread. Thread was up to my chest. I struggled to push through the flood of thread, but my body tangled more & more into the thread. I knew I couldn't break the thread. If I broke the thread, I'd never find a way out of the hospital.

*

The dark moved on the ceiling. The ceiling smiled & twitched its lips. My invisible friend was by my bed. I got up & put my hand in his hand. His hand was big tonight. He only had a thumb & two fingers. Fresh scabs were the other fingers should be.

He grew taller beside me until his hand pulled out of my grip. He turned to me & poked his thumbs into his eye sockets. He pushed his eyeballs all the way in & then pinched his eyelids & when he pinched his eyelids his eyes disappeared into a blank whiteness of face. He was ten feet tall. His back arched & bent against the ceiling. The ceiling twitched & licked at him. He pinched his nose closed & his nose disappeared. His face was a whiteness with a wide red mouth.

His body was a woman's body. Meaty breasts on his chest, sagging & sliding like eels. His hips were wide & thick hair grew like shadows between his legs.

His fingers were hot & wet. They rubbed against my body. They pushed me down on the bed & took my clothes off me. They squeezed my thighs & pinched my stomach & pinched me & pinched my cheeks. I didn't want him to disappear my eyes & nose. I didn't want him to steal my face. If he stole my face he'd be me & Dad would think he was me.

I spun away & hid beneath the bed. His blank white faceless face was there under the bed beside me. His breasts wriggled over me & pressed me into the floor. He opened his mouth & leaves & dirt & twigs poured out, poured out like water in the bathtub. The leaves & twigs wrapped around me. It smelled like trash cans. I kept my mouth closed, but the dirt slipped in through my nose & wedged my mouth open & then everything went into me & everything was dark.

*

My uncle had been sleeping on the couch. Each morning he folded the sheets & covers into a neat pile beside the couch. Each day he went to the hospital to see my dad. Ever since Dad had laughed & then choked I hadn't been to the hospital. I hoped the thread was still in the hallways, unbroken. I hoped my uncle would not break the thread.

When my uncle found the dog he screamed. Mom ran outside. I watched them through the sliding glass door. It looked like Mom was standing with another version of Dad. He was kneeling in the ground, holding the dog's body up. Mom shook her head like there were bees. Her eyes closed so tight I worried they'd disappear. She covered her face, but when she moved her hands away, her mouth was still there.

My invisible friend put his finger over his lips & whispered "Shhhhhh." He beckoned me with his finger to the bedroom. He lifted my pillow up & showed the bloody kitchen knife under the pillow. I pushed the pillow back down.

I heard the sliding glass door open & then close. Then Mom was on the phone. Through the walls, Mom gurgled like a drain.

My invisible friend hugged me. He held my face between his hands. He pushed his face in. I was afraid he'd steal my face but he kissed me on the lips, the way they kiss in movies. As he kissed, his lips slid inside me, then his cheeks, his nose, his whole face slid into my mouth, until he was gone & inside me.

*

I woke & walked into the kitchen to get a glass of water. Pushing the stool over to the sink I climbed up & turned the faucet on. Red poured from the faucet. I tried to turn the faucet off but red kept pouring out. It filled the sink & spilled over the counter & onto the floor. The floor covered in red. The red reached out to the living room where my uncle was snoring. I didn't want it to reach the carpet.

Then the red rose up from the kitchen floor. It formed a column & the red column turned into my dad. Dad reached a red hand out toward me, palm extended. I walked toward him, red splattering over my toes, up my bare legs. He put his red hand to my cheek, but the hand splashed apart when it touched me. Then Red Dad collapsed into a red whirlpool with arms & legs.

The red whirlpool pulled at me. If I was pulled into the whirl-pool I would wake with no face & somewhere out there in a hospital with no way out, a little boy would be born with my face.

*

I woke & walked to the kitchen to get a glass of water. The light was on in the living room. My uncle sat on the couch with a bottle & a glass in front of him. He looked tired & round.

"Come here," he said.

I did not approach him.

"Come here, Mike," said.

"That's not my name," I said.

"OK, OK. Come here, kiddo" he said. I walked to the couch. His eyes were red.

"Can't sleep?"

I didn't say anything.

"Me neither, little man."

He put his hand on the top of my head. His palm was heavy & moist.

"It's a riddle," my uncle said & pulled me to him on the couch. He sat me on his lap & wrapped his arms around me. "We bury things & bury things, & then we have to keep burying the same things."

In his arms it smelled like night in the dirt. He put his chin onto the top of my head & the bristles scratched my scalp.

"But you can never bury anything deep enough, can you Mikey?" he asked.

"That's not my name," I said. I pictured his arms forming a box around me, the wooden box in the bedroom closet, the box in which I store all my toys.

*

My invisible friend cut a hole in his chest & reached into his chest & pulled a bone out. Red covered the bone. The bone white beneath the red. He handed the bone to me. Warm & sticky. I put the bone beneath my pillow, beside the crusted knife.

My invisible friend reached into his chest again & pulled another bone out, handed it to me. Then another & then another, another. I hid each bone beneath my pillow, until the pillow towered high over the bed & red stained the bed. His chest was thin now & the skin flopped & billowed as he breathed.

He reached into his mouth & pushed his fingers up between lips & teeth. Pushed up his face, beneath the skin, until he hooked his thumb under the upper jaw & pulled his skull right out of his mouth. He held the skull to my face, red & glistening. White eyeballs twirled wildly in the sockets. His face collapsed onto his chest like a deflated balloon.

*

We lay deep in the underbrush. I had my imaginary friend's bones in my red pillowcase. His loose face lay over my face, his loose chest flat against me. I could feel his little heart twitch & thump, his slack lungs suck weakly in & out.

In the woods The King of the Wood searched for us. It had Dad's body, but gigantic, & a thousand antlers grew off of every part of the body, clacking & gnashing & grinding & shattering as it ran.

When the King of the Wood came near us, crushing stones & logs beneath its hooves, ripping out small trees & bushes, the bones in the pillowcase rattled. The King of the Wood stopped & listened, snorting through my dad's nose. It raised its face to the night sky, stretched its arms up, antlers cracking & ripping out of its skin, & howled, loud as fire alarms.

The rattling bones in the pillowcase whined & chirped, rubbing like cricket legs. The King of the Wood stumped slowly to where we lay in the underbrush. It bent over us. Chunks of antler splintered & fell like hot hail. He inhaled deeply, the whole night sucking into his black mouth. Then he bellowed into the earth. My ears stilled & rang. The underbrush blew off of our bodies. We were naked & bare to the night. The stars speared through the trees spines. My invisible friend leaking into my face, my body.

The King of the Wood reached for me. His palms were covered in tiny antlers like a plant's spines. He held my chin in his hand. Tiny antlers poked through my skin. The antlers entered me, grew into me.

When I opened my eyes the King of the Wood was gone. My invisible friend was gone. My pillowcase was red but empty. I touched my face where my dad had held me & felt tiny antlers growing from my skin. The tiny antlers pierced my soft fingertips & began growing inside my fingertips.

*

I woke & walked to the kitchen to get a glass of water. The light in the living room showed my uncle on the couch with a bottle & a glass on the coffee table. His eyes were red & black spots with no light moving inside them. Stubble grew from his face & I remembered its needle scratch.

I sat on the couch beside him. He turned his head. He was holding his mouth tightly shut, as if holding something back. There was no red on my hands. My pajamas were clean. At night like this, tired & afraid, he looked just like Dad.

"Do you need a glass of water?" I asked.

My uncle closed his eyes tight.

I walked to the kitchen. Pushing the stool over to the sink I climbed up & turned the faucet on. I filled my plastic mug with water & walked back to the living room.

My uncle stood at front of the couch. His eyes & mouth squeezed so tight his face was bright red. I offered him the water, but he could not see me. I turned the mug so the handle extended & touched the handle to his hand. Dad's face. His eyes sprang open. Red & black. He opened his mouth & dirt & twigs & roots poured out, showering over me & entangling me, itching & scratching my skin, knotting my arms & legs tight. The twigs & roots entered my mouth & filled my mouth & pushed down my throat. My stomach filled & burst open & the roots poured from my stomach, soaked in red. They pushed through my skull. My eyes popped from the sockets. I was lifted. The house broke apart around me, broken open by the roots. I rose into the cold night until the starlight entered me. I was the breath that breathes when all things are dark. I was the mouths of leaves.

NEW ORLEANS

You are in the hospital, hooked up to machines. Machines beep & click & buzz: a language you can almost, but not quite, translate. You want to text a friend, but they've taken your phone. In your phone's place, they left a flip-phone. The edges of the flip-phone are rough, unsanded, made cheap in the factory of worn-out machines. You flip it open. Instead of a screen, there is a shiny steel marble. In the marble's curved surface you see the whole room reflected, distorted & liquid. In the distortion of the reflection there is something you need to learn, something important in the wobble & reach of the steel marble's surface, but you don't know what. You reach a finger toward the marble, & your finger grows large, takes up almost all the reflection. You touch the marble & you are on a carousel. The carousel spins fast, wind whipping clothes against your body. You cling to the ornately carved horse. All around you, others cling to their horses & lions & squirrels & zebras & catfishes, all laughing, some releasing one hand to feel eminent danger, to tempt danger. To fall from one of these carousel animals at this speed would be certain death. Slowly, finger by finger, you loosen your grip on the horse. You release one hand. You feel a kind of freedom, an understanding rising from no longer needing. All the carousel riders cling to animals by one hand. And then, ahead of you, a woman in a wedding dress releases her other hand. The speed flings her from her armadillo. She flies backward, screaming, but not in fear. Then another releases their grip & flies off their tiger. Another flies off his giraffe. You open your eyes into the piercing wind of motion & let go. The air lifts you from your horse & you are the tailor at a stately old hotel, measuring a man for a suit. You assemble the suit right onto his body, cutting excess cloth with a razor, sewing seams around each curve & length of him. *So where you here from?* you ask. He's a big man, tall & wide with muscle. *California*, the man says. *Oh*, you say. *I like California. What part?* The man laughs a little breath of a laugh. *Los Angeles*, he says. *Ohhh!* you say. *How exciting. Do you ever run into movie stars there?* The man shakes his head. *Every day*, he says with a laugh. *It can be exhausting.* You sew his suit tight, completing the final seam. *OK*, you say. *How does it look?* The big man turns this way & that in the mirror. The suit fits his thick body how morning fog slides over a coastal mountain. It is a one-day suit, sewn so perfectly he will never be able to remove it, will tear the seams open to remove the suit. *It's perfect*, the man says. You fix a few tiny spots. Cut a couple spare threads. The man takes out his wallet & pays you in cash. As he walks out the door into the busy sidewalks of pedestrians, you notice that the man is Dwayne "The Rock" Johnson. On the street, The Rock is immediately stopped. Strangers ask him to take selfies with them beneath the hotel sign. An anole runs up your leg, up your side. You raise one arm. The anole runs up to the tips of your outstretched fingers. The anole flaps its front legs frantically until the legs flatten, turn into wings. The anole rises into the air, flapping its flattened legs. You watch the little lizard fly up, up, to the open skylight, out the skylight & you are a small storm cloud, full of sudden thunder & wildness. You float over the city, drenching one block with rain, then holding the rain in on the next block. You rain on tourists & they run for cover. You rain on locals & they lift their faces up to let rain caress their cheeks. You hold the rain in until you swell like a toad. You hold the storm in, ballooning, nearly to the bursting point, holding all the storm inside you & then you are in the attic of an ancient mansion. The attic is full of jewelry & gold coins & silver jugs. All the silver is tarnished, the jewelry crusted. This is the booty of history. The forgotten treasure of centuries of various oppressions. Among the treasures, grubs & worms squirm & wriggle. Tiny armadillos roots through the piles of riches. The armadillos push their noses into the coins & rings & necklaces, indifferent to the wealth, licking up the grubs & worms & the War of 1812 never ended, they just kept the war secret all these centuries at it continued & a man on a horse rides up to you & hands you a letter. You break the wax seal & open the letter. You have been drafted into the secret war. Because the war is secret, you can't tell anyone you've been drafted, & you can't act like you've been drafted. The only people who can know are you & this man on the horse & whoever wrote the letter. A man walks out of a dumpling shop with two orders of dumplings. You've never seen this man before, but you know he is the man who wrote the draft letter. And he knows you know who he is. The man who wrote the draft letter hands you an order of dumplings. The two of you walk to a busy square & sit on a bench. A person on a wooden crate sings songs, sad songs, sung like someone digging a grave in dry dirt with their fingers, The singer strums a broken chunk of a dismantled piano. *Nice weather we're having*, you say to the man who wrote the draft letter. *If you don't like the weather, stick around ten minutes*, he says. That's secret code for something, but you don't know what. You finish your dumplings & get up & walk down a quiet street on which a fig tree grows over the sidewalk. The fig tree is so overgrown that you must push your way through the thick & gnarled branches, careful not to knock ripe figs from the tree, the unctuous scent of figs filling the air, & as you push through the overgrown branches, the foliage blots out the sun & it grows quiet & cool within the overgrown fig tree. You push through tangles of overgrown branches, sliding your body into the open spaces, pressing through narrow gaps, the interior of the fig tree's branches like a labyrinth, pushing through the fig tree for so long you forget what day it is, what city you are in. You forget your story. Forget your name. You are what moves through the branches of the fig tree. Each space between branches appears as a revelation, like a gasp, like a heart that beats so slowly one could live & die & be reborn between two heartbeats. You reach the center of the labyrinth of the fig tree & you are a child, playing with other children in a dirty drainage ditch that you all refer to as "The Creek" & someone yells out "snake" & then the other children all yell "snake" & so you yell "snake" & all of you climb out the drainage ditch, dirty water dripping off dirty clothes & you all pick up stones & throw the stones into the ditch to hit the snake. You don't see a snake but everyone is yelling "snake" & throwing stones & you too are yelling "snake" & throwing stones, so there must be a snake in there, there has to be, or what's the point? You walk away from the drainage ditch, the "creek," walk toward the church. As you approach, the church reveals itself to be three churches, each one identical & you find a bundle of money on the ground of the parking lot. The bundle is all one-hundred dollar bills, but the expiration date on each of the one-hundred dollar bills is yesterday's date. You figure that maybe the money is still good. You go to Robert's & you load the grocery cart up with groceries & push it to the register. The person at the register rings up the groceries. *One hundred & eighty-seven dollars*, the person at the register says. You hand them two of the one-hundred dollar bills. The person holds the bills out, far from their body. *I'm sorry baby, but these bills went bad yesterday. You see?* They say, & hold up the bills. The bills are as loose & floppy as an untickleable dick. You consider arguing your case, that the bills might still be good, to test them, but the bills are so droopy there's no argument to be made, & then you are driving down St. Claude when your car clunks & shakes. Smoke rises from beneath the hood. You pull into an empty lot & turn the car off. Black smoke billows when you open the hood. A farmer sits at a wooden table, watching you. The table is covered with turnips. The farmer beckons you over. As you walk to the table, it's farther away than you'd thought—the turnips are so huge it created an optical illusion. As you get close to the table the turnips tower over you like Neolithic standing stones. The farmer is the same size that he looked from afar. *Your car's not working*, the farmer says. *My car?* you say. *That your car?* the farmer says, pointing to your car, now engulfed in flames. *No way*, you say. *That's my car.* You point to a shiny blue El Camino. You walk to the El Camino. The door is locked. You try the key from your burning car. It unlocks the El Camino. You try your key in the El Camino ignition. The El Camino starts with a roar. You drive out of the empty lot, waving at the farmer & his enormous turnips. The farmer waves back. You pull out into the street & then a single limpkin flies over your head & then a single great blue heron flies over you & then a single egret & then two wood ducks & then two black-belly ducks & then a single orange-crowned warbler & then a single anhinga & then a single bald eagle & then a single barn swallow & then a single pileated woodpecker & then a red-breasted theorem flies over your head & then a flaming treehouse flies over you & then an Atari cartridge flies over you & then a rich cloud of the dense smell of roasting coffee surrounds you, so fragrant you can see the smell & floodwater rises up your calves. The floodwater is so full of fish that there's very little water to the floodwater, mostly fishes crammed against fishes & smaller fishes wriggling into spaces between the bigger fishes & even smaller fishes wriggling between the smaller fishes & to get out of the flood you step into Anna's & walk right back to the bathroom. You look in the bathroom mirror, through the tags & stickers & graffiti, & see a four leaf clover growing out of the bottom of your chin. Everything shifts perspectives, suddenly flips, so that the clover is growing straight into the air & you are now upside-down. You follow the four-leaf clover's life, the daily dramas & exults of bees & sunlight, the reckoning with the brevity of a life rooted in a chin, the hard-fought joys & profundities a clover finds in this mixed-up modern world. You feel creepy watching this clover's dream, so you quietly sneak out of the clover's dream & to the bar. The bartender places a tumbler before you. *If you drink of this*, the bartender says, *you will love like a lover of the Elizabethan era.* You sip the concoction. It tastes new-car-smell taste. The bartender places a second tumbler onto the bar. *If you drink of this, there will always be room.* You sip the concoction. It is as bitter as an overcrowded room. But in the bitterness, through the heart of the bitterness, you can taste a spacious room. The bartender places a third tumbler onto the bar. *If you drink of this you...* You turn away before the bartender can finish. Everyone in the room is dressed in formal jacket & tie & gown & tiara. Faint piano pings & echoes down long hallways of marble & mahogany. A metal chair lies sideways on the marble floor. You lift the metal chair & it comes apart in your hands. The screws all loose. You pull a screwdriver from your pocket & screw the metal chair back together. The people in suits & gowns watch you work, silently & attentively & then you smash your El Camino into the wide trunk of an ancient tree. You are unharmed, but the El Camino is totaled. You open the car door & realize you & the tree & the car are inside the State Supreme Court building. The El Camino bursts into flames. Men & women in suits & dresses & uniforms pass you & the burning car, undisturbed by the wreckage, giving the scarred tree only a passing glance & you climb up the levee & the river is red with cinnamon, scent of cinnamon filling the city & then you are online, clicking buttons on an old angelfire website for the City of New Orleans on which animated cartoon men with hats raise & lower their arms in alarm, waving at you, trying to get your attention. You click the button that says CLICK HERE & you are in a new boutique hotel that is an abandoned warehouse. Rich people from all over the world travel to the abandoned warehouse hotel for a guided & authentic experience of squatting in an abandoned warehouse, though with reverse-osmosis filtered water on tap & with an small-plate restaurant & you are chatting with a cyprus tree at a bar that floats in a swamp. Your fingers slowly slide across the wet knuckle of one of the tree's protruding roots & then you are out by the highway & you walk up to a VW van parked behind a busy gas station. You cup your hands around the windows & look inside. Inside the van there is a desert & in the middle of the desert sits an oasis, a small blue pool surrounded by palm trees & then you are on a roller coaster that runs through Bourbon Street & there are parts of Bourbon Street no one has ever seen, that can only be seen from the vantage point of this roller coaster. The unseen parts of Bourbon Street fit between the parts that can be seen, eternally present, eternally hidden. In these unseen places, a New Orleans no one has ever seen thrives, people with unnamable names feeling emotions no one has ever felt. History & time entwine like a bed of rain on which anyone might discover a new continent, like a storm cloud you could swallow in a single gulp that lasts the length of an unlived life.

PHASE CHANGE

I knock on the front door. No answer.

A note sticks out under the door: *UNLOCKED — UPSTAIRS — MASTER BATH*. And the final word, twice as large & jagged: *HURRY!*

I try the handle. As the note claims: unlocked. Inside is unlit but moonlight shows the hardwood floors & mcmansion furniture. Nothing happens when I flick the light switches. This house, like so many others I've delivered to since the fires, is dead, but a thick sound buzzes through the walls.

I return to my truck & lift four of the twelve insulated bags from the bed, carry two on each shoulder. The houses on the block are all dark except one on the corner with candlelit windows.

In my flashlight beam, the first floor looks messy in that way kids make everything messy, but not ransacked. Dishes in the drying rack beside the sink. I rub my finger across a glass & trail a clean line in the dust.

There's a bad smell & I follow it into a dark pantry. A plastic dog pen as tall as my knees. Dried blood splatter rings outside the pen's grate. Bits of dried flesh stick to the grate. Two dog claws, like busted moons, sit on the tiled floor. Inside the pen is a still & stinking darkness. I don't shine my light inside.

Upstairs, something thumps, then a noise like a voice.

The house is warm & damp, but as I climb the stairs I feel the cold. The cold slips down along the steps like liquid. The buzz buzzes louder. Buzzing through my legs, quivering the bones, the marrow.

I follow the cold & the buzz, both from the same side of the house. I try the door at the end of the hall. It opens, just so, then resistance. I set the four bags down & put my shoulder into it. Rugs bunch back as the door gives way & the door exhales a wave of frozen air. The buzz is now a thick & constant growl. The hair along my arms rises. My skin of my face tightens.

The windows are covered with plastic trash bags, held down with duct tape. In the spotlight of my flashlight, the black mass covering the floor reveals itself to be human remains.

The bodies had been ripped open, into pieces, flesh ground into the carpet, left to cake & dry into one mess. At least two heads, one adult with some curly hair massed beside it, one head smaller. Could be another head in the corner.

I want to run, to escape, but I can't go yet. I'm the delivery man. I have a job to do. People depend on me. A duty.

I wedge the rugs back further & retrieve my bags, stepping sideways to fit through the door.

The buzzing, chest-shaking, comes from the door on the far side of the bed. I have to walk over the caked mass on the floor to reach the bathroom door. My footsteps crunch. Some parts are sticky as fresh asphalt.

I hold the handle for a moment. The icy metal vibrates like an engine. I close my eyes & open the door.

The cold presses against me, brings tears from my eyes when I open them. Two generators, pushed far back into a deep linen closet, are the source of the crushing buzz. This close the buzz trembles my cheeks, chatters my teeth. Orange electrical cords weave out from them to air conditioners wedged into the four windows, held in place with towels & duct tape, the edges taped off in thick haphazard layers.

From the tub, full to the lip with murky water, a man emerges, naked & bright with cold. His fingers blue, genitals cringed tight into him, eyes sunken & ringed in black.

The man exclaims wildly, holding his hands up in fists. The grind of the generators is so loud I can't hear what he's shouting.

I set the four bags down & slip my gloves on. Unzipping one bag I pull the chunk of dry ice out, lifting with my legs. The man leans close. The haze rises off the ice to caress his skin. I sense him restraining himself from rubbing his face against the block. Bathwater drips off his nose onto the dry ice & dances & pops into fog, its squeal audible beneath the roar of the generators.

His cold hands circle my arms. The fingers trembling & twitching. I can smell it — the musk, that stink of my father. My father leaning over me in the garage to grab a tool from the rack. My father's arm reflexively pushing me back as he jammed the brakes in his Ford truck.

He leans close. His breath hot against my ear.

"We lived on flowers," the man says. "No rain."

He smiles. His teeth white against the blue lips. The cold of his fingers sting my skin. I pull my arm from his grip. On my arm, he leaves a residue of pink.

The man stares at the pink residue. The water in the bathtub continues its slow slosh. Water drips off his elbows, his nose. As the cold water drips off his fingers it splashes red on the white tile floor.

For a slow few seconds, he watches his fingers drip away onto the tiles. His palm, where he had held my arm, is runny as undercooked egg. What I took for bathwater on his face is the arrested motion of his skin melting away. I feel the cold then, surrounding me, a body pressed against me.

The man lifts the smoking hunk of dry ice. The slopped skin of his hand firms against it, the tips of his fingers wedged flat. He moves to drop the ice into the bath & for a single hesitating moment the block of ice doesn't fall, adhered to the frozen drippings of the man's fingers. Then, decisive, it rips the tips of his fingers off & plops into the tub.

Fog courses from the bubbling howling of the ice exploding into gas. Milky carbon dioxide fills the room. I unzip the remaining three insulated bags &, wearing my insulated gloves, remove the ice & set it on the tile floor.

The fog is so thick I can't see anything. It feels like paper towels in my throat. I know the man won't live long in this fog. But what can I do? I am the deliveryman.

I exit the bathroom & as I close the door the grind of the generators quiets. My steps again break through the blackened crust of bodies. I scan my flashlight across the framed family photos that line the stairwell. Three children, apparently.

I close the front door. The handle clicks. I have one more delivery & already it's getting dark. The smoke from the fires light yet another stupendous sunset, shrill with pinks & reds. I must get home before dark. My wife knows not to unlock the door after dark, not even for me.

THE PREGNANT COUPLE

A woman had been pregnant for almost two years. The day after the anniversary of her due date her husband became pregnant as well. It happened all at once. One day he was a skinny man with a skinny man's pointy beard. The next day he was completely pregnant, his breasts distended & wide.

It is a lucky thing to have a pregnant woman in one's village, so the villagers had been happy about the woman's long pregnancy. However, no one could decide if a pregnant man was lucky or unlucky.

The pregnant man complained about the pain in his back & how his breast milk leaked & soured inside his coat. He spent more time now with his wife, huddled together on the couch, whispering things to each other they immediately forgot.

The mayor of the village visited the pregnant couple. There had been a meeting of the villagers & they requested he go straighten things out.

"What are you planning to do?" asked the mayor.

"I'm not certain," the pregnant man responded. "This has all been quite sudden. I think I will remain pregnant for a while longer & make my decision then."

"Do you know," asked the mayor, "if it is lucky to have a pregnant man in the village?"

The man did not know, but he was worried about the repercussions if they thought him unlucky, so he told the mayor that it was the luckiest thing of all to have a pregnant man in one's village because it was so rare.

The mayor left & the pregnant man & his pregnant wife went to bed, but the pregnant wife found that she could not sleep. The baby inside her was kicking & turning about so much that it kept her up. Finally she decided that the only way to get some sleep was to give birth to the baby.

The woman woke her husband up & told him that she wanted to give birth to the baby. He put some water on to boil & fetched the clean towels from the closet & he called their midwife who said she'd be over in twenty minutes.

As the pregnant couple waited for the midwife they watched a little TV. It was late so there were mostly just reruns. They watched an episode of a Law & Order in which a preacher had killed his wife & claimed god made him do it. Sam Waterson was just about to turn the preacher's god against him when there was a knock on the door.

The midwife was at the door, but the mayor was as well, which was a surprise.

"Her car woke me up," the mayor said, "So I figured I'd come over & see what was happening." He seemed a little tipsy.

The pregnant woman got some drinks for the midwife & the mayor & put some coffee on to percolate. Then she set herself down on the living room floor in order to give birth. Her husband began to get jealous, though, & he decided he wanted to give birth then as well. He set himself up on the floor as well.

The mayor refilled his drink. He was getting pretty drunk. The midwife sat between the two pregnant people.

The pregnant couple began to give birth at the same time, but at the moment when the babies were about to come out the mayor drunkenly tripped over & fell between them & they accidentally gave birth to the mayor. Then, since she was no longer pregnant, the woman went to sleep.

After that the mayor had to move into their house & they had to raise him up. It was difficult at first because all the books they had about raising babies were designed for small babies rather than adult babies. It was difficult for the mayor as well, because he needed to suckle at the breasts of his mother & father. This behavior does not endear one to voters.

HEARTS

My mother had a heart of gold. She died when I was twenty-one years old. I had a heart of stainless steel. Sometimes when I ran & it beat fast, it rang like a small bell.

My oldest brother had a heart of aluminum. My next-to-oldest brother had a heart of brass. My little brother had a heart of lead. It was so heavy it was difficult for him to move. When he shifted too quickly inertia caused his lead heart to sway in his chest & he was left breathless & confused.

My father had a congenital heart defect. A wide pink scar bisected his chest, looking slick & wet. His chest had been opened so many times that the bones in the center of his ribcage were no longer fused together. When he went in the water he couldn't dive deep or his chest would pop open from the pressure.

At my mother's funeral my oldest brother greeted all the relatives. We'd told her siblings they needn't make the trip in—they'd been here just the month earlier to visit her in the hospital—but they did. Her brother & two sisters sat in the front row of church pews as the pianist played somber music for the arriving mourners. Her brother had snuck in a coffee that smelled like anisette. My oldest brother made everyone feel welcome. When he shakes your hand his hand bends to fit around yours.

My father sat with his twin brother, the one with the healthy heart. They'd looked identical as kids but as they'd grown, one healthy & one sickly, they'd veered away from each other. Now, aging, with my dad's gout & blood pressure, my uncle's shot liver, they were beginning to look identical again. I had taken care of the details for the funeral. The priest & I had planned the songs & readings. I'd met with the crematorium to arrange for her remains. My next to oldest brother had accompanied me & scowled silently, arms crossed over his chest.

During the funeral my little brother sat in the far corner, his skinny body propped against the wall. His clothes, somehow always too big, dripped off his frame, his shirt coming undone, his tie slack.

After the ceremony we put the box of ashes into a hole in the memorial wall behind the church. My dad had bought two adjacent slots.

After all the crying & the sunlight, it was just him & us brothers standing there. He leaned against the memorial wall. He rubbed his fingers across the cut letters of her name & the dates.

"This is where I'll go," he said, touching a finger to the empty slot next to hers.

It was only about six months later when my father died. His weak heart finally gave out. One afternoon when I went over to borrow his drill I found the garage open, the hood of his Chevy up & him slumped over the cold engine.

The church was less full for my father's funeral. His brother was in the front row but my mother's siblings had not flown in. My father had only gone to church to keep my mother happy & had ceased entirely after she died. Some elderly women whom I took to be regulars sat in the middle of the room, though there were many open pews in front of them. At the potluck meal afterwards one of them approached me, her plate laden with fried chicken & pasta salad, & expressed her deepest sympathies for my mother's passing.

After my father died my brothers & I drifted further apart. We are not great talkers, any of us, & had mostly learned about what was going on in each other's lives through my mother. At holidays we'd get together & watch things on TV & talk about what movies we'd seen. On birthdays we'd ring one another or we wouldn't & none felt the worse for it either way.

When I told women I met at bars that both my parents had died recently I thought it made me seem ungrounded, like anything was possible. I was young then. I didn't know what families were for. One woman, sipping the gin & tonic I'd bought her, said, "So you're an orphan?"

"Not exactly," I responded. That night she held me after we had sex. She asked me about my parents & I gave noncommittal answers. I wanted her to feel sorry for me because I liked the way she held me, but death just felt like one of those things you have to do. Like going to Target. Cleaning the toilet. She laid her head on my chest & listened to my steel heart beat.

"It's like a jackhammer," she said. "I like the little clanging." She was silent for a bit longer & then said, "No, it's more like a watch, one of those old-fashioned watches where you can hear the machinery at work along with the tick tock."

"TickTOCK, tickTOCK, tickTOCK, tickTOCK" she muttered, repeating this until it made me sleepy. She had long straight hair & I liked how it felt splayed out over my skin.

"Ask me what time it is," she said.

"What time is it?" I asked her.

*

When my little brother called I didn't know what to say. I hadn't talked to him since his birthday the previous year, about a month after our father died. We'd both forgotten to call on each other's birthdays this year.

His hair had fallen out, he told me. The doctors figured out that the soft metal of his lead heart had ground off & gotten into his bloodstream.

"They figure that's why I've been in & out of the hospital so much this year," he explained.

"That makes sense," I said, but I'd had no idea about the hospital visits.

He needed to have a heart transplant. He was going to have it done in North Carolina where I lived. My parents had moved here because they had the best hospital for heart work & my father's doctor had recommended it. I'd moved with them, my little brother too. We were still in high school. I'd gone to college in New York City but moved back down afterwards. I work in computer design. My little brother had gotten a full scholarship to a liberal arts college in Ohio, but due to his condition, he'd dropped out after a semester. Because of embarrassment or inertia or whatever, he'd stayed in Dayton, working a series of underachieving jobs that he'd lose or quit due to his perpetual sickness & lethargy.

He wanted a favor. He wanted to move in with me, into the

guest room in my apartment, while he was preparing for the surgery. It'd be a few weeks before he was admitted into the hospital but they had a lot of tests to do. He called them "prelims."

"Of course," I told him, because that's what you do.

He'd warned me, & I'd seen some photos online, but I was not prepared for the changes. The baldness was one thing, I had friends who shaved their heads. But the way his bones pushed against his skin was something else, the bones some- how wispier as they became more pronounced. That was un- expected.

The first night here he came out of the shower with a towel wrapped around his waist. I could see not only his six-pack of scrawny abs, but every single muscle feature on his chest & stomach. There wasn't an ounce of fat on him. The towel wrapped around him completely twice.

We went shopping the next day. He carried a list the doctors had given him of ingredients to avoid & we spent our time reading the backs of boxes like scholarly collectors.

His eastern medicine doctors had given him a separate list of herbs & oils & teas to get & we had to go to the hippie co-op for that. My little brother wore a stocking cap over his bald head, but he looked pretty fucked up. As he was discussing the things he had to buy with a plump assistant in the soaps & medicines section, she teared up & asked him if she could hug him. He said yes & stood awkwardly as she wrapped her bare arms around him, touching her hands to her elbows behind his back. She had thick, curly hair tied back behind her head. Even at a distance I could smell her cedar smell.

After she let him go she went to the back room to find a few items that they didn't have upfront. "You two should get a room," I joked.

My brother didn't respond. Tears ran down his face. The sickness had made his eyes bug out & they were strained & red.

I turned & looked at the handmade soaps. I held one to my nose. Then another. I gave each one a good sniff. Each was complex & earthy. Each cost ten bucks a bar. When I looked back at my brother he'd wiped the tears away.

*

At first my oldest brother didn't think he was going to make it out, but my next-to-oldest had agreed immediately. I wanted all of us to be together when my little brother went into the hospital for the surgery. A week before that, my oldest brother sent me a text that read "My schedule shifted. Can make it! Woot woot!"

I called him immediately but he didn't pick up. In the message I told him I wanted him to stay with me but that he'd need to bring a sleeping bag & a pillow. I had an airbed in addition to the guest room, but I didn't have bedding.

Five minutes later he texted me back: "Dnt worry. Katrina in Chapel Hill. Will stay w her."

Katrina was an ex of his. He'd proposed to her & then broken it off. It had messed her up pretty bad but she remained devoted to him. Every time he was between relationships he'd return to Katrina. They'd go on some trip, scuba diving with manta rays, a week in Southern France, always some kind of package deal that could be bought in a rush. Each time he'd ditch her when he found someone else.

I called him again. He didn't pick up. I told the voicemail that I wanted him to stay with me, that it was important for him to stay with me.

A few minutes later he texted back "Cool!"

*

The airport shuttle pulled up & my next-to-oldest brother got out. He had a carry-on suitcase that rolled. I'd been waiting outside the apartment building since he'd texted a few minutes ago, smoking a cigarette & thinking about him. I'd never seen him smile. He was always at the edge of becoming annoyed or angry but he never actually got angry. When he was younger that scowl got him in trouble at bars. But he was a thick, tough guy & could get away with mostly anything.

He hugged me & I hugged him back, both of us using only one arm & slapping the back.

"When did you see him last?" I asked.

"Yesterday, I guess," he said.

"Yesterday?" I asked.

"On Facetime," he said.

"You Facetime?" I asked. My voice had pitched somewhat high.

"Why is that such a surprise? He & I Facetime two or three times a week," he said.

"Three times a week?" It had never occurred to me to Facetime with any of my brothers. "What do you two talk about?"

"Nothing really. TV. Mom & dad," he said. "He tells me about what he's cooking. He's been using mom's crock pot a lot lately."

"Mom had a crock pot?"

I'd never used a crock pot. I wasn't really sure what one was.

We ordered pizza. I'd been doing the vegan thing for a little while but I didn't feel like talking about it, so I just went ahead & ate the cheese.

Someone had brought the DVD of *Road House* & we started it up while waiting for the pizzas. My little brother & my next-to-oldest brother talked about movies & TV shows I wasn't familiar with. It was like they were picking up an interrupted conversation. They made fun of my small TV. I tried to keep myself from saying that I hated TV, but I said it a few times.

The pizzas arrived. We ate & then I put the plates in the sink to wash them in the morning. I offered beers but both of them waved them off. I drank one & then another, but they just gave me a headache. My little brother retired to the guest room & I blew up the airbed for my older brother with the little motor.

Before I went to bed I was doing one last check of email & facebook. My little brother had changed his status to "Pain don't hurt."

I liked it.

*

"If I make it through this OK then I think I'm going to get that tattoo." my little brother told me on the way to the hospital. I wasn't sure what tattoo he was talking about, but I encouraged him to do just that.

My oldest brother had missed his flight the night before & took a cab straight from the airport to the hospital. My next-to-oldest brother & I were in the waiting room, killing time between magazines & our phones. The doctors had taken my little brother in about an hour earlier. He had perked up once he had the hospital gown on. He was talking fast & smiling with his teeth.

I heard my oldest brother's laugh before I saw him. He was on his cellphone, yelling into it. I was instantly annoyed. He walked in a circle just beyond the waiting room seats for about twenty more minutes, talking to someone he kept calling "babe."

Once he clicked the phone off he sat down next to me with a huff. He smelled citrusy.

"Where's your bag?" I asked him.

"Didn't bring one," he said.

A doctor came out about fifteen minutes later —far too early. As he approached us, I decided that my little brother was dead. Therefore nothing the doctor would say could upset me.

"We've run into a bit of a snag," the doctor said. "Perhaps we should have assumed something like this would happen, considering your family's history."

My older brother stared at him. His arms were folded & his forearms looked like hairy tree trunks. My oldest brother smiled at the doctor & nodded.

"Is he—" I paused. "You know, passed away?"

"No. Not really. It's not as simple as that," the doctor said. "I think you'd all better come with me."

He led us into a spare room with children's toys piled in the corner. He pulled up two swiveling office chairs & one stool. My oldest brother sat on a chair & swiveled slightly back & forth. I sat on the stool. My next-to-oldest brother stood, arms crossed.

When they cracked my little brother's chest they'd found that his heart was no longer a leaden thing. Instead there was a jar full of keys where his heart should be. The doctor showed us a few photos on a laptop screen. The first showed the jar covered in blood & grime. For the last few they'd wiped it off a bit & removed the lid. In all the photos, the bottom bit of his intubated face showed, his lips slack & blameless.

"So it's not lead poisoning," the doctor explained. We were still facing the laptop screen, though we were no longer talking about the photos. My oldest brother was looking at the pile of children's toys & bouncing his knees.

"So what is the plan?" my next-to-oldest brother asked the doctor.

"Well," said the doctor, watching my oldest brother walk over to the pile of toys & begin to poke through them, "We're a bit stymied. It's got to be one of the keys causing all of this, but we can't figure out which." He turned back to the photo on the laptop. "It could be more than one of the keys, even. Do you recognize any of these?" he asked us.

The keys were anonymous. No skeleton keys or fancy ornate ones. No clunky office building keys. Just normal keys for common doorknobs.

"That one sort of looks like our old house key," I said. "But then again, it looks like my apartment key as well."

My oldest brother held up an old toy police car, the kind that you roll backwards & it speeds forward. "Check this out!" he said. "I used to have this same car, except it was a taxi!"

"So you need to remove at least one of the keys," my next to oldest brother said.

"Yeah, in a perfect world," the doctor said, "we could figure out which one it is by swapping them out & charting his re-actions."

"What do you mean by a perfect world," I asked.

"One where we could crack his chest open every day," the doctor said.

*

For the next week we went to the hospital every day. My little brother was pretty drugged at first then he wasn't. As before, he was more spirited in the hospital.

"Keys!" he said when the doctor explained the situation. "I wondered what all that rattling was. Must be a lot of keys for it to be as heavy as the old lead guy."

"Yes, the jar was filled right to the lid," the doctor said. He chuckled, as if talking about an old shared joke.

The next week my older brother had to return home & to work. The week after that my next-to-oldest brother had to go as well. He promised to be back immediately if there were any changes. He made me promise to call him every day & I agreed, though I hate the phone.

Then it was just me visiting every day. We'd watch TV togeth-er, *Law & Order*. The hospital only got like twelve channels but there was always a *Law & Order* marathon on one.

One day I was there, at the snack machine getting Doritos (I'd given up on the vegan thing), when suddenly I was on the floor & there was a nurse kneeling over me. I could see right down her cleavage. She was an older woman, maybe late fif-ties, but she had large breasts & while I normally don't stare like that, it was all I could look at. I laughed & she said "You back with us?"

Then the laugh turned into a cough & then I was just cough-ing. Unable to stop.

The doctor who'd explained the key situation happened to be on hand that day. He stopped in while another doctor was checking me out.

"I think we should get an echo of his heart," the doctor said to my doctor. "You know his family, right?"

"Yep," my doctor said, both of them ignoring my presence in the room. "He's the brass heart, right?"

"Steel," I said.

"No," said the other doctor, "He has the steel heart."

"Right, right," my doctor said. "Well we need to get him in there quick, there's nothing beating here at all."

"Interesting," the other doctor said.

"I know, right?" my doctor said.

The next day three doctors hovered around the screen as an echocardiographer rubbed her tool around my chest. They muttered to one another, quietly so I couldn't hear, but they were baffled.

"Could it be?" one doctor said.

"I think so," said another, "but I've never seen this before."

The echocardiographer changed the angle a bit & all three doctors sighed.

"Yep," said the doctor who'd been taking care of me earlier, "That is definitely an apple."

"An apple?" I said, but no one heard me.

*

That night, back in my apartment, I cooked up some broccoli & brown rice. I sat down in front of the TV, my food steaming. The basic cable gave me forty-three channels. I scanned through the channels, looking for something to watch. The news shows had too many crazed graphics running across the screen. The game shows were glib. The laugh tracks too loud in the sitcoms. Dramatic pauses too prolonged in the dramas.

I wanted something specific, a particular feeling, a particular escape. When I was in college I'd planned to do a lot of traveling. I'd wanted to backpack across Europe, to swim in the clear waters off the coast of Thailand. PBS had some show with the camera sweeping over the icy mountains of Antarctica.

I laid my hand over my chest. Nothing was beating there. I touched my fingers to my throat. No pulse. The food had cooled on the table. I scrolled through the names in my contacts list, looking for the right person to call & tell them about my heart, but I couldn't find anyone to call.

THE ANDROMEDA STRAIN,
A NOVEL BY MICHAEL
CRICHTON

Robert could not stop quoting *The Andromeda Strain*, a novel by Michael Crichton. He read the book every day. It was the only book he'd read since he was seventeen; he was now thirty-six. He had the book memorized, even the copyright page. He liked the book very much, at first. His bookshelf looked a little like this:

```
TTTTTTTTTTTTTTTTTTTTTTTTT
HHHHHHHHHHHHHHHHHHHHHHHHH
EEEEEEEEEEEEEEEEEEEEEEEEE

AAAAAAAAAAAAAAAAAAAAAAAAA
NNNNNNNNNNNNNNNNNNNNNNNNN
DDDDDDDDDDDDDDDDDDDDDDDDD
RRRRRRRRRRRRRRRRRRRRRRRRR
OOOOOOOOOOOOOOOOOOOOOOOOO
MMMMMMMMMMMMMMMMMMMMMMMMM
EEEEEEEEEEEEEEEEEEEEEEEEE    D
DDDDDDDDDDDDDDDDDDDDDDDDD    I
AAAAAAAAAAAAAAAAAAAAAAAAA    C
                            T
SSSSSSSSSSSSSSSSSSSSSSSSS    I
TTTTTTTTTTTTTTTTTTTTTTTTT    O
RRRRRRRRRRRRRRRRRRRRRRRRR    N
AAAAAAAAAAAAAAAAAAAAAAAAA    A
IIIIIIIIIIIIIIIIIIIIIIIII    R
NNNNNNNNNNNNNNNNNNNNNNNNN    Y
```

The dictionary had belonged to his mother.

Given his commitment to *The Andromeda Strain*, Robert had difficulties. It was difficult, for instance, to talk to anyone who wasn't constantly thinking about *The Andromeda Strain*. And it was difficult to talk to those who were, as they had all been sullied by the film. Robert had never seen the film.

One day Robert was leaving his job at the bakery. He'd been tired & had moved slowly during the night & consequently did not finish until dawn. Normally no one was out this early in the city, but to his left he saw a priest. The priest was wearing one of those long black cloaks that covered him to his feet. Because he had that burst of energy he always had when leaving work & because the sunrise was particularly pink, Robert decided to follow the priest.

The bakery was on 33rd Street. Robert followed the priest to 25th Street. At that point the priest turned around & stared at Robert. Robert stopped. He looked down at his feet, kicked at the sidewalk. An orange cab drove by slowly, the driver peeking over to see if either of the stopped men needed a ride. The priest turned around & began walking again. Robert followed.

After another two blocks the priest turned around & walked toward Robert. Robert stopped & waited. When the priest arrived he asked, "What are you doing?"

"For years it was stated that men had forty-eight chromosomes in their cells; there were pictures to prove it, and any number of careful studies," Robert said.

"Why are you following me?" the priest asked.

"For years it was stated that men had forty-eight chromosomes in their cells; there were pictures to prove it, and any number of careful studies," Robert said.

The priest stood still for a moment, looking directly into Robert's eyes. Then he made a little noise, an exhalation. Then the priest punched Robert in the throat. Robert doubled over, gasping for breath. The priest pushed him onto the ground. Robert curled into a fetal position. The priest kicked him twice in the back, below the ribs where the organs lie.

The next night Robert took extra care shaping the baguettes & sat down for a while before beginning the muffins, absently touching his tender throat. When it was nearly dawn he washed the dried dough off his hands & forearms, tossed his apron into the dirty-apron sack & stood outside. Not seven minutes later the priest walked by.

Robert called out, "This man apparently survived the night. He was the one walking around when the planes flew over, and he was still alive this morning."

The priest turned to look, recognized Robert & with a sigh walked back toward him. Robert held his hands up in front of him & took a step back. "This man apparently survived the night," he said.

The priest approached Robert & as he got close he grabbed the back of Robert's head & jammed it down into his rising knee. Robert fell to the sidewalk, dazed.

The following night was one of his days off, but Robert, his eye swollen & purple, again awaited the priest at dawn.

When the priest spotted him Robert fell to his knees with his hands raised. "No, this isn't a hospital," he yelled. Though his eyes were closed Robert heard the approaching footsteps thudding. He fell to the ground & held his hands around his head.

But Robert did not feel the expected kick, in fact, the footsteps passed by him. Without moving out of the fetal position,

Robert opened one eye. Down the block he saw the priest pummeling another man who was lying on the sidewalk.

Curious, Robert rose & walked down toward the two men, though he tried to remain silent so as not to attract the priest's attention & violence. As he approached he thought that the man being pummeled looked familiar, but he could not quite place him. Just then the priest ran off, turning left on Lafayette.

Robert reached the pummeled man & was surprised to find that the man looked identical to him. He reached a hand down to help the pummeled man up, but the pummeled man only looked back at Robert, not extending his own hand.

"What's going on here?" the pummeled man asked.

"How do you feel now?" Robert said. Gripping him by the shoulders, he helped the pummeled man to his feet. Looking at the pummeled man's face Robert felt suddenly woozy. The man was the same height as him, his hair was cut in an identical style & he had the same face. It was not unlike looking into a mirror. The pummeled man had blood running out of his nose & did not have a swollen eye.

"What's going on here?" the pummeled man asked again, brushing the sidewalk dirt off his clothes.

"How do you feel now?" Robert responded again, unsure of what he should do in this situation.

"Man, you could be my twin," the pummeled man said.

"That is correct, sir," Robert said.

"You see that priest? He jumped me. A priest! You ever seen anything like that?" the pummeled man said.

"There were no further transmissions," Robert said.

The pummeled man rubbed his red cheek & looked Robert over, lingering on the flour-whitened cuffs of the navy work pants. "You a baker?" he asked.

"'Yes,' Leavitt said. He frowned." Robert said.

"I used to do that a bit myself, back when I was in school," the pummeled man said. "Night job. I was tired all the time."

Just then an orange cab appeared down the block. The pummeled man raised his arm & the cab pulled up & over to the curb.

"Where you headed? We could share this," the pummeled man said.

"It's just impossible for me to say. We must wait for the findings of the investigative committee," Robert said. But he did not approach the cab.

"Yeah well," the pummeled man said after an awkward moment, "you watch out for that priest." He opened the cab door but then looked back at Robert. "It really is eerie," he said.

The next night Robert arrived at the bakery just as the day employees were finishing their closing routine. As usual, they smiled at one another, waved, & did not speak. Robert pulled the white trash cans filled with flour & whole wheat & rye from under the table & removed their tight tops.

He put in his favorite baking CD, disc seven of the unabridged reading of *The Andromeda Strain*. He poured warm water, honey & yeast into the mixer & let it sit. The front lights turned off, signaling the departure of the day employees. Robert measured out the flour on the scales. Then he walked over to his backpack & removed a glass jar. He put the jar in a white bucket &, with one of the wooden spoons, smashed it into tiny slivers of glass. He poured the glass into the mixer with the flour & set the machine to medium.

The stereo said, "Stone, watching the screen, said, 'More light.'"

Robert pressed the red button that turned the stereo off.

I BOUGHT A SWORD

One day I decided to buy a sword. I got on eBay and looked up swords. I didn't know so many people were selling and buying swords. Some of those swords, you wouldn't even believe it.

I found a few nice swords. Most were out of my price range. There was one, though, that looked really cool and didn't cost too much. It looked like the kind of sword you'd think of when I say "think of a cool sword."

I'm not sure what I thought I was going to do with the sword. I just pictured myself swinging a sword and thought "Yeah. That."

I put in a bid for the sword. A few days later an email told me I'd won the auction. I paid the guy. A week later the sword arrived.

The sword turned out to be magical, of course. But I didn't know until later. Mostly I was just into having a sword. I'd never owned a sword before. I've never even owned a knife, other than the ones in the silverware drawer. No guns. I don't even play those kinds of video games.

I made my bed and put the sword on top of the blanket. I took a photograph of the sword like that and posted it on

Facebook. Some of my friends liked the photo and comment-
ed "cool sword!" or "bad ass!!!"

The next time I talked to my sister she said "Did you buy a
sword?" I told her I had. She didn't say anything else about
the sword.

My sister was trying to find a new job. She said that she was
underutilized at her current job. I said, "That sucks."

She said, "You know? It really does, Matt."

Sometimes I think about winning the lottery. I like to imagine the first thing I would buy. Usually I imagine buying
something like a boat. If I had a boat I could just sail around.
I'd have to learn to sail, but they must have lessons for that.
But if I had a boat. Like a boat with a cabin and a stove. What
else would I need?

The sword didn't look right on the shelf and my apartment
doesn't have a fireplace or mantle. I hammered some nails
into the wall and hung the sword up, but it was so heavy it
cracked the drywall. They'll probably take that out of my de-
posit when I move out.

I'm not a belt guy. So I had to go out and buy a belt in order
to have a belt to tuck the sword into. I bought a pretty good
belt from TJ Maxx. Thick, thick leather.

When my buddy Richard came over, I showed him the sword.
He touched the tip with his thumb and cut his thumb.

"That's really sharp!" he said.

"Sharp as all get out," I said.

There were some band-aids in the bathroom, but by the time
I got back with one, the bleeding had already stopped.

Richard had me take a couple pictures of him holding the sword. He looked really cool holding the sword. He did this thing with his face that I've never seen him do before. He looked glorious. Everybody looks cool holding a sword. That's the whole point of a sword.

I told Richard that he should buy a sword. Then we can both have swords.

He said, "Maybe."

Later that night we put some pizzas in the oven and scrolled through Netflix. It took us a while to agree on a movie. Once the movie started, we both just looked at our phones. Richard posted a picture of him holding my sword onto Facebook. I told him to put that I took the photo, and he did. He got more likes than my picture of my sword. But whatever. I don't think about that stuff.

Work that next week was terrible. I had so many meetings, you wouldn't believe it. And by the time the weekend came, I was exhausted. By Sunday morning I needed to get out of the apartment. I hadn't stepped foot out the front door since I'd gotten home Friday. I decided to drive out to the national park. I love it out there.

At the last minute, like just before I was about to go out the door, totally out of nowhere, I grabbed the sword. I didn't have one of those things for it, a holster, so I carried the sword just like a sword. I hid it with my body, in case anyone was looking out their windows.

The park was almost empty. Just me and the mountains. I kept looking out the windows, hoping to see a bear, but no dice. I pulled off to a gravel spot and parked. I got out and stretched my back. The air felt so good. Everything was so clean. Sometimes when I'm out in places like this, I just get happy, like the real kind of happy. I sucked in a deep breath, as deep as I could and held it until my lungs began to hurt. I grabbed the sword from the back seat. A dirt trail led from the gravel parking area through some trees and into a big field. I walked down the trail, with my sword.

Once I got to the big field, with the mountains behind me, I thought "This is a cool place to swing my sword." So I swang my sword. The sword swang through the air and suddenly things felt all weird. There was a big woosh, a woosh of gravity or something, the whole of everything expanding and contracting, and suddenly I was on the field of battle.

It was crazy.

They were guys in full-on knight's armor battling big monsters with green skin. There were archers shooting arrows at the monsters too. There was clanging, shouting, roaring, and everything. There were dead bodies on the ground. One knight screamed and ran in circles, holding his arm. His hand had been bitten off. I think the monster must have eaten his hand. I was just looking around, like "Whoa!"

Then this big monster ran up, bigger than the other monsters. He knocked the head knight down. All the other knights stopped and watched, jaws dropped. The monster rammed one foot down onto the knight, crunching his armor like it was a beer can.

"Hark!" the knight said, staring right at me. "It is time for you to meet your destiny! It is time for you to plunge into battle!"

"Oh man," I said, "I don't know."

"You hold in your hands the immortal blade of Azan Azakke," the knight said (I don't know if I'm spelling that right). "As the bearer of such a magical sword, it is your duty to battle evil." The monster pressed down harder. The knight's armor squeaked. He cried out in pain.

The sword was doing something weird. It buzzed in my hands, like it was electric. The sword pulled me. Its sharp tip drew toward the monster. I walked toward the monster with the sword, but the sword pulled me forward until I was jogging, then running. I ran right up to the monster and swang the sword. Though it felt like the sword was swinging itself, that I was just holding on.

The sword slipped through the air with a musical noise and sliced right through the monster, cutting through his muscle and even his bones. It cut him right in half. The top half of the monster fell off of him. Blood went everywhere. You could see the stuff inside him. His body slumped to the ground. He actually landed on the knight. It took four of us to roll his body off.

I guess because this monster was the biggest monster, all the other monsters got scared after I killed him. They all ran away. The archers kept shooting arrows at the fleeing monsters, catching some of them.

The injured monsters screamed in pain. I know they're monsters and everything, but they sounded so horrible screaming in pain. It was worse somehow than the injured knights, because the monsters don't have any language, so all they could do was scream.

We collected the dead. We put the dead monsters into a pile and burned them. There was a cart pulled by a bunch of horses to carry off the dead humans. I don't know where they went.

I thought maybe, since I'd killed the monster, they might make me king. But there was already a king. He was cool. He had a great beard. He had me sit right next to him during the feast in my honor. He called me a hero. I kept being like "I don't know if I'm a hero, really." But they insisted. I wasn't into their food. Except for the desserts. Everyone called me Sir Matthew, even though I told them to just call me Matt.

They gave me a holster for the sword. Though they called it something else. And they gave me a really nice belt. I already told you, before, that I'm not a belt guy, but this belt I most certainly made an exception for.

After that, most of the king's people left. I stayed at the castle with a few of the knights. They were cool, but they all had known each other since they were kids and I didn't get their jokes. I asked if I could do anything to help out around the castle, but there wasn't much for me to do. Some of the knights would travel out and return, reporting back about this or that. I thought maybe I could do something with my skills, since I was from the future, but nothing came of that. I told the knights all about computers and they all thought they sounded great.

After a few weeks, the head knight—the guy I'd saved—told me that it was time for me to return to my world. This shocked me. I didn't know I had to go back. I told him that I didn't want to. I liked it there.

"Sir Matthew," he said, "you came to us in our time of need. You heroically defeated the Weevklve." (Spelling, again.) "But you are not of our world and there is no hope for happiness for you here." I told him that I was actually much happier here. I tried to explain how bored I was back in my world, how boring my apartment was. But he said that if I stayed away from my world my body would soon fall apart and I would die, so I guess that settled that.

The next day a wizard guy cast a spell and sent me back. Even though weeks had gone by in the other world, I was returned right at the moment when I left, my hands still in mid-swing with the sword. Back in that field. The mountains filling up the horizon to the west. Purple and yellow flowers in the grass. It was beautiful there. Really beautiful. I swang my sword around some more. But it didn't feel right.

I kept waiting for them to bring me back. There must be other monsters I can kill. I went to the park all the time at first, and any time there wasn't anyone else in that parking spot, I'd take my sword out to the field and swing it around. I thought maybe that would trigger it. I tried going to other parts of the park and swinging my sword around. Then other spots. I saw a lot of great parts of the mountains around then, trying out new spots. But none of them worked.

I think about it sometimes, being whisked away to some magical land. Like when I'm in a meeting and someone's being really awful, or when I've done something wrong, I think about the fact that I fought a monster and defeated it. I did that. But what do you do with that? It's not something I can post about on Facebook. I mean, my mom would see that.

I looked up boats for sale on the internet one night. Boats are really expensive.

I haven't been out to the park in a while now. I don't even feel like going there anymore. When I drive by signs that point to the park, I get a weird feeling inside, like that feeling you get in your face when you're about to cry. But I get it in my stomach, where I can't cry. Sometimes I chant some nonsense words, or I scream like one of the injured monsters. Sometimes I punch myself in my own thigh, one knuckle out, charley horse style.

I know I could do something great out there again, if they would just let me.

The belt they gave me is too fancy to wear around here. But I bought some stuff from Home Depot and made a frame in which to display the belt and the sword. The frame, with the sword, belt, holster, and everything, is too heavy to hang up so I lean it against the wall on top of my dresser. When Richard came over and I showed him the belt, he was pretty impressed. I thought about telling him about the monster and everything, but I didn't. I don't know why not.

EGGS

When she was only a small child, a violinist signed a contract with a recording company. She was so young that her talent had not yet fully developed. The contract allowed the executives of the recording company to each year assess the progress of her talent & decide whether to record & release her music. She was not, the contract strictly dictated, allowed to record music or perform in public until the recording company assessed her talent as "Progressed."

In her youth, the violinist prepared for the annual assessment as one might for a standardized test or religious ritual. Daily practice, complete mental & emotional focus. But each year after her performance the record executives smiled kind smiles & told the violinist sincerely & profusely that she was very good, but that her talent had not yet fully progressed.

Each year, the record executives, not wanting to look heartless, gave the violinist a consolation gift. Each year the record executives gave the violinist an enormous yellow egg. The violinist then had to take care of each enormous yellow egg & keep it healthy & safe. Each egg was as big as a pubescent boy.

Each year a man in a blue suit drove the violinist home from the assessment. Through the windows familiar houses & buildings passed, the auto-body shop, the press club, the busy marina, the boarded-up school, the less-busy marina, the empty lot where vines & small trees grew through rusted grocery carts. Each year there were more grocery carts.

Over the years, the violinist attempted various approaches— one year a perfect rendition of a Schubert sonata, the next year atonal avant garde music, one year a traditional folksong & the next year music of her own creation. One year the violinist prepared by practicing a single piece each day, one thousand times a day. The next year she never practiced & fished for trout each day, then improvised during the assessment. But the result was each year the same: the record executives complimented & thanked her sincerely & profusely, so sincerely & profusely that for a moment each year she thought this year might be the year. But then the record executives, as they did each year, assessed her talent as not fully progressed. And then, before parting, a man in a blue suit carried in a large gift box tied with a velvet ribbon. The violinist then opened the gift box, which contained an enormous yellow egg.

As the violinist grew older & older, her apartment filled with yellow eggs. She bought a house & the house filled with yellow eggs.

As the violinist grew into adulthood & middle age, fewer record executives attended the annual assessments as they died off one by one.

One year the violinist arrived for her annual assessment. Her assessments had been held in the same building each year since she was a child. The building was a comfortable Victorian house, the rooms remodeled into practice spaces, foam padding covering the walls. The air had a specific scent of old wood & lemon cleaning agent. The violinist associated this specific scent, without having ever identified the emotion, with a specific emotion.

The violinist opened the door to the practice room in which the annual assessment was held. Inside sat only one old record executive in an electric wheelchair, aged & wizened, hands shaking. The record executive smiled at the violinist. The violinist, as she did each year, positioned herself at the front of the space. She took her sheet music from her bag & placed it on the cold metal music stand. She held her bow above the strings, took a deep breath, exhaled, & began to play. She played the solo from Ernest Chausson's *Poème*. It is a sad piece of music, & it is in E-flat minor, an awkward key. It is sad & it is difficult.

The violinist finished. Her eyes were closed. She had not, though the piece is difficult, needed the sheet music. The strings scuffed as the violinist removed the bow. She kept her eyes closed. The room was quiet. A stuffy quiet. The violinist grew suddenly afraid the old record executive might have died. But when she opened her eyes the record executive was alive & alert in her electric wheelchair. Tears shined on the record executive's wrinkled cheeks.

The record executive nodded. She held her shaking hands together & lifted them up from her lap. She was attempting to raise her hands to applaud, but was unable to. The violinist understood & was touched.

"Thank you," the record executive said. "Thank you for your beautiful performance. Thank you for your work & your commitment to your talent. Thank you for the joy you have brought me each year during these assessments." The record executive's appreciation was sincere & profuse.

"When we began this life together," the record executive said, "there were many record executives. Each year we looked forward to the annual assessment of the progress of your talents. Each year we savored your performance. But each year we recognized that your talent had not yet fully progressed, that though you were delightfully talented your talent could yet continue to progress."

The violinist stood beside the metal music stand, holding her violin in one hand & her bow in the other. She did not know what would be the outcome of the old record executive's speech & she was interested & hopeful.

"I am the last of the record executives," the record executive said. "There will never be more record executives. Our time is over. We were a dying breed & soon we will be extinct."

The violinist began to say something, but the record executive lifted a single shaking finger.

"Do not mourn us," the record executive said. "Nature has its way & its truths. But I need you to know that I will not be here next year. I need you to know that these moments with you each year have been the joy I have looked forward to most deeply. I have fallen in love & I have fallen out of love. I have been disappointed & I have been rewarded. I have seen many things of sublimity & awe. But they were events. They occurred & they disappeared. And in memory I have only a caricature of the events, a cold cadaver of joys & sorrows."

"And so, soon I will be dead. Next year there will be no record executives to assess the progress of your talents. I'm repeating myself—I apologize. I do that these days. Next year, it will be up to you to decide whether you will come to this room & perform. There will be no disadvantage or penalty if you do not. After I am dead, your contract will be terminated."

The old record executive looked up to the corner of the practice room, where the soundproof foam had discolored from beige to grey.

"I hope you will. I hope you will arrive here & stand at the front of this room & perform. I hope you will, though there will be no record executives present to assess the progress of your talent. I hope you see why your performance here is essential."

The old record executive then pressed a button on the side of her electric wheelchair. The door opened & the man in a blue suit carried in a gift box & set it before the violinist. The violinist placed her bow into her violin case & placed her violin in. She shut the case & closed the clasps. She took the sheet music from the metal music stand & put it into its folder & put the folder in her bag.

The violinist grasped the end of the velvet ribbon & pulled it. The ribbon fell to the floor. She held the sides of the gift box lid & lifted it. She placed the lid beside the box. She pushed the tissue paper aside & revealed the large yellow egg.

"Thank you," the violinist said to the record executive. "This is a very kind gift." The record executive nodded. The violinist placed the lid back onto the gift box. She placed the velvet ribbon in her bag alongside the folder containing her sheet music.

Outside, the man in the blue suit, as he did each year, opened the trunk of the blue sedan & put her bag & her case & the giftbox into the trunk. He opened the back door of the blue sedan. The violinist entered the sedan & reclined into the soft cloth seat. She watched the city pass through the windows, this city she barely recognized any more, with its block-long batches of white condos with clean corners & its skyline filled with spinning cranes & scaffolding.

Once back at her house, the man in the blue suit carried the giftbox into the house, while the violinist carried her case & her bag. She offered, as she did each year, the man in the blue suit tea or coffee. He, as he did each year, smiled & shook his head, pointing to his watch.

The only room in the violinist's house that contained furniture was her bedroom, in which she slept & undressed & dressed & practiced her violin & read the occasional novel or magazine & did her sewing. The rest of the house was filled with the enormous yellow eggs, each sitting on a small pillow that the violinist had sewn herself. The violinist lifted the newest yellow egg out of the giftbox & wandered through the house, stepping around the eggs.

The enormous egg was very heavy. The liquid within the egg shifted awkwardly as the violinist moved. But over the years she had grown used to this awkwardness & walked with her feet splayed out. She held the egg with both arms bent beneath it. She lifted with her legs, not with her back.

The violinist searched for a spot to place this newest egg & found one in what might be, for another resident of the house, the TV room. She placed the yellow egg down in the empty spot & stared at the yellow egg & considered what kind of pillow she would make for it.

END GAME

The ringing echo of gunshots faded among the stone walls of the church. The air smelled iron from all the blood, but also gamey, something old. He kept pulling at the trigger, though the gun was empty. He dropped it. Blood dripped into his eyes. He wiped at them, but his fingers were coated & he only rubbed more blood in. He ran his hands up & down his chest, around his head, along his arms, looking for wounds, but he could not find any. With all that gunfire, so many shooters, how could he not have been hit. Nothing hurt except his aching jaw, & that was from that other thing last night.

The man stepped over the bodies & walked up the altar steps, the marble slick with blood. He walked back into the sacristy. Stripping off his clothes, he stood before the full-length mirror, twisting to examine himself. The freshly blood-stained skin of his face offset against the white skin where the clothes protected him. Still, no wounds.

In the hallway to the rectory, the bodies of two women crumpled together into a heap. He passed them without looking to see if she was one of them.

In Father John's room, he opened the closet & took a pair of khakis & a blue oxford shirt, laying them on the bed. As he bent, drops of blood dripped from his hair onto the shirt.

In the shower he scrubbed blood from his skin. He filled his mouth with hot water & spat out pink. Even the steam smelled like blood. He washed his hair, then washed it again. He turned the cold water down until he could barely stand the heat. His calves flexed involuntarily. He stayed until the steam smelled only of lavender shampoo.

He dried off & returned to Father John's room. From the closet he took a Brooks Brothers shirt with stiff collar & cuffs. The tag was still on the shirt. He ripped that off. The shirt was baggy on him, as were the pants.

Father John's wallet was on his dresser, next to his keys. He took both. In another priest's room he found a pair of running shoes that fit. In the kitchen he packed a tote bag with apples, a loaf of bread, some salami & a box of cookies. There was no soda, only small bottles of water. He took those.

Behind the rectory, he tested the Chrysler key on the matching cars. It opened the third one. Black, of course. All the church cars are black.

The church parking lot was still. Cars had been abandoned haphazardly & he had to weave through them to the exit. A few bodies lay twisted among the cars, others sprawled inside the cars, the windshields like red carnations gone brown. To avoid driving over one body, he pulled the Chrysler into the grass. The undercarriage scraped on the high curb.

At the exit, he paused. Right or left? He looked first in one direction & then the other. Then he turned left.

He drove past the neighborhood pool where he & his brothers had done swim team, had been lifeguards, where someone had stolen his first & only skateboard. He drove past the high school, where he'd seen a boy punch another boy over & over again until he was unconscious, while no one stopped him. The school lot was empty.

A strip mall of Asian markets & pool halls, all the lights now dead. The old diner where he used to sit for hours drinking coffee with his friends. The neon sign still lit: Tastee 29. In the distance, toward downtown, the smoke hung in thick, deliberate clumps.

He passed the turn toward home & instead headed to the highway. The gas tank read just above empty. He stopped at the Shell. It was empty but the pump was automatic & still worked. He slid his card in. The digital readout authorized it. He stuck the nozzle into the tank. A car drove by slowly, a Subaru hatchback. The driver stared. He stared back. The Subaru slowed to a stop, waited, then pulled a squealing u-turn & sped away.

The man capped his gas tank & got back in. A wallet of CDs was wedged between the front seats. He chose John Denver's greatest hits & turned the volume up. At the highway he went north, then west, then north, & then west again on the empty interstate. He set the song "The Eagle & the Hawk" on repeat. It was too short & he needed to keep hearing it. A weird burst of yearning among the bland pop-folk: "I am the hawk & there's blood on my feathers."

As he drove west he began to see cars. East coast license plates. One or two people in the car. Some back seats packed with camping gear & boxes, some empty. They stared at him as they passed, or he stared at them. That one song on repeat: "All that you can be & not what we are."

Eventually the plates turned local. The drivers no longer stared. Fields of soybeans, green as paint, stretched into distance, broken up by shaggy corn. He drove through the night, stopping only for gas, eating & drinking only what he'd taken from the rectory.

At dawn the sky flushed pink. The plains opened around

him in every direction, infinite & anonymous. He turned the stereo off & opened the windows, all four. The wind twined through the car, slapping the loose shirt against his chest, buffeting the stiff collar against his neck.

He exited the interstate. Ahead of him an old pick-up truck drove slowly. He nudged the breaks to slow behind them. A girl, maybe eighteen, sat in the truck bed, facing him. The wind swirled her hair into a great black halo. She held it from her eyes with one forearm.

He followed the car to the end of the exit. Then pulled over a lane to pass it.

The girl with the black hair raised her right hand & waved. The morning sun was yellow & viscous behind her. She smiled. He lifted one hand from the steering wheel & waved back..

Acknowledgments

"The Man Who Married a House" appeared in *Noo*. "Lake" appeared in *Twelve Stories* & then again in *Another Chicago Magazine*. "The Photographer & the Very Tall Man" appeared in *Birkensnake*. "The Pregnant Couple" appeared in *Matchbook*. "School" appeared in *The Collagist*. "Phase Change" appeared in *Kill Author*. "My Father is a Disappearance" appeared in *Pear Noir*. "My Arm" appeared in *Timber*. "Hearts" appeared in *Unstuck*. "Eggs" appeared in *The Mississippi Review*. "The Andromeda Strain, a Novel by Michael Crichton" appeared in *Black Warrior Review*. "Train" & "New Orleans" were first published as zines I did for the Dream Delivery Service. "I Bought A Sword" I posted entirely on Twitter during the early days of the Covid-19 pandemic because I thought that was funny at the time.

Deepest thanks to Nate Perkins for bearing with my anxieties & being so supportive.

Eternal love to Julia Cohen. Without her, this book would not exist.

Mathias Svalina is the author of nine books. *Comedy* is his first short story collection. Svalina was a founding editor of the small press Octopus Books, & since 2014 he's run a Dream Delivery Service, traveling around the country to write & deliver dreams to subscribers. With the Dream Delivery Service, he's worked with the Denver Museum of Contemporary Art, the Poetry Foundation, & the MOCA Tucson. His current home base is Richmond, Virginia.

With a Difference
by Francis Daulerio and Nick Gregorio

Western Erotica Ho
by Bram Riddlebarger

Las Vegas Bootlegger
by Noah Cicero

The Green and the Gold
by Bart Schaneman

Selftitled
by Nicole Morning

The Only Living Girl in Chicago
by Mallory Smart

Tourorist
by Tanner Ballengee

Until the Red Swallows It All
by Mason Parker

Dead Mediums
by Dan Leach

Let's Walk Together
by Elva Ambía Rebatta & the Quechua Collective of NY

www.tridentcafe.com/trident-press-titles

9 781951 226244